"Oh, *neh*, I'm all thumbs," Eliza said...

"I tied my basket on too tight, but I think it's in a knot, so I can't loosen it. Could you please help me with it, Jonas?"

But then it occurred to Jonas that she was *flirting* with him.

"Sure, I'll give it a try," he said. As he loosened the knot, he was close enough to lean forward and whisper in her ear, "I'm sorry I didn't get to see you yesterday, but may I take you for a ride next *Sunndaag* after *kurrich*?"

"I'd like that a lot," she whispered back, turning her head ever so slightly. Her face was so close to his that if they'd actually been courting and no one else had been around them, he might have been tempted to kiss her cheek.

The unbidden thought was so disquieting to him that Jonas stepped back and said to her brothers, "If your teeth are *bloh* when you *kumme* back, I'll know what you've been eating!"

Carrie Lighte lives in Massachusetts next door to a Mennonite farming family, and she frequently spots deer, foxes, fisher cats, coyotes and turkeys in her backyard. Having enjoyed traveling to several Amish communities in the eastern United States, she looks forward to visiting settlements in the western states and in Canada. When she's not reading, writing or researching, Carrie likes to hike, kayak, bake and play word games.

Books by Carrie Lighte

Love Inspired

The Amish of New Hope

Hiding Her Amish Secret
An Unexpected Amish Harvest
Caring for Her Amish Family
Their Pretend Courtship

Amish of Serenity Ridge

Courting the Amish Nanny
The Amish Nurse's Suitor
Her Amish Suitor's Secret
The Amish Widow's Christmas Hope

Amish Country Courtships

Amish Triplets for Christmas
Anna's Forgotten Fiancé
An Amish Holiday Wedding
Minding the Amish Baby
Her New Amish Family
Her Amish Holiday Suitor

Visit the Author Profile page at LoveInspired.com.

Their Pretend Courtship

Carrie Lighte

LOVE INSPIRED
INSPIRATIONAL ROMANCE

LOVE INSPIRED®

INSPIRATIONAL ROMANCE

ISBN-13: 978-1-335-75928-3

Their Pretend Courtship

Copyright © 2022 by Carrie Lighte

Recycling programs for this product may not exist in your area.

For questions and comments about the quality of this book, please contact us at CustomerService@Harlequin.com.

Love Inspired
22 Adelaide St. West, 41st Floor
Toronto, Ontario M5H 4E3, Canada
www.LoveInspired.com

Printed in U.S.A.

Forbearing one another, and forgiving one another, if any man have a quarrel against any: even as Christ forgave you, so also do ye.
—*Colossians* 3:13

For every reader who has encouraged me
with generous, uplifting feedback—thank you!

Chapter One

"Sit down, Eliza. Your *mamm* and I have something important we want to discuss with you," Uri Gehman announced.

Eliza Keim could guess what her stepfather was going to say. Every summer since Eliza turned eighteen, he'd given her a different version of the same lecture. "It's time for you to get married and start a *familye* of your own in a *haus* of your own," he'd say. "I should be planting extra celery in my garden by now."

It was the beginning of July, more than two weeks past the time of year when young courting Amish couples in New Hope, Maine, informed their parents of their intentions to get married during the autumn wedding season. In turn, the couples' families planted extra celery because the vegetable was an essential ingredient in traditional Amish wedding meals. But for the fifth year in a row, Eliza hadn't approached her parents about increasing the size of their garden. Uri was aware that she'd been seeing her latest suitor, Petrus Kramer, since last July, so he undoubtedly wanted an update on the status of their relationship.

No one else I know is expected to discuss their courtships with their eldre, Eliza silently brooded.

In fact, most couples she knew went to great lengths to keep their romantic relationships a secret from their peers, as well as from their family members. There were exceptions, of course; some young people were pleased to make it known they were courting. But Eliza was not one of them and she resented having to discuss the subject with her stepfather. However, even though she was twenty-three years old and even though Uri wasn't technically her father, Eliza respected the Biblical commandment that children honor their parents. She slid into a chair at the kitchen table.

"Aren't you going to sit with us, too, Lior?" Uri asked Eliza's mother, who was presterilizing jars in preparation for putting up strawberry preserves.

Can't he see she's busy? Eliza marveled to herself. Clearly, the timing of this discussion wasn't her mother's idea; she probably hadn't wanted to discuss the subject at all. But Lior hesitantly wiped her hands on her apron and took a seat beside her husband. Uri didn't waste any time getting to the point.

"We've been expecting you and Petrus to speak to us about your intention to marry," he said, the gruff tone in his voice matching the expression on his face. "We understand that he's up north in Fort Fairfield for the summer. Is that why you haven't spoken to us yet?"

"Neh." Eliza glanced down at her hands, folded atop the table, so she wouldn't have to look Uri in the eye.

"Petrus and I aren't getting married. Our courtship ended before he left."

Petrus had been deeply disappointed when she'd told him she didn't want him as her suitor any longer. Like Eliza's stepfather, he'd assumed that after almost a year of courting, they were on their way to marriage. *But she'd been very clear from the beginning that accepting him as a suitor didn't mean she was seeking to get married. She distinctly told him she'd like to get to know him better as a friend before they could even consider a romantic relationship.*

During the entire time they'd courted, Eliza had only walked out with Petrus on three or four occasions per month at most. And when they had socialized together, she'd always made a point of suggesting they participate in group outings, such as hiking or bowling with their peers. The only time they'd ever been alone was during their travel time in his buggy.

And although Eliza was a warmhearted person by nature, she'd been careful to never voice any special sentiments toward Petrus. And she'd certainly never allowed him to hold her hand, much less kiss her. In essence, she'd treated him as if he was a brother. A favorite brother, perhaps, but nothing more. So he'd had no reason to believe marriage was on the horizon for the two of them.

Still, when he'd brought up the topic a few weeks ago, Eliza was pained to discover how optimistic he'd been about sharing a future with her. That was why she'd broken up with him; she didn't want to give him false hope that if they continued courting long enough, she'd develop romantic feelings for him and eventually agree to become his wife.

Uri was drumming his fingers against the table, signaling he was impatiently awaiting an explanation, so she elaborated, "I didn't believe we were a *gut* match."

"In what way?" her stepfather asked, causing Eliza to draw back her head in surprise. Even for him, the question was intrusive.

"Uri, if she says they weren't a *gut* match, we should trust her judgment. Eliza's almost twenty-four. She doesn't have to ex—" Lior began to defend her daughter's privacy, but her husband cut her off.

"That's right. She's almost twenty-four. She should be married by now. She should be raising her own family in her own home. And if she doesn't intend to get married, she ought to find a full-time job and contribute to our *familye's* expenses."

"But she already contributes to our expenses and I need her help here," Lior objected.

"Three of the *buwe* will be in *schul* all day once it begins in September," Uri pointed out to his wife. "So you'll only have two at home with you."

Eliza's five half brothers were three, four, six, eight and nine. While it was true that it might be a little easier for her mother to manage because six-year-old Samuel would start attending school in the fall, Uri clearly had no appreciation for all the effort it took to keep their household running smoothly. Especially since the youngest boys were also the most active of the bunch. And Lior struggled with low energy, which her doctor attributed to having a baby when she was forty-two and then another at forty-three, in addition to the three sons she was already raising.

"I could increase the number of rugs I make. Or increase their size so I could charge more for them," Eliza suggested. She consigned handmade rag rugs at the local Amish hardware store and then gave seventy-five percent of what she earned to her family's needs, ten percent to the needs of the church and the other fifteen percent she kept for herself. Her stepfather had never complained about this financial arrangement before now.

He ignored her offer and continued to harp on the topic of her courtships. "Every time you break up with a suitor, you give the same reason—you don't believe you're a *gut* match. It seems like it's a matter of *hochmut* for you to reject one suitor after the next."

Hochmut meant pride, and to be fair, Eliza could understand why Uri thought she was acting as if she was somehow superior to her suitors. But she honestly hadn't been rejecting any of *them*; she'd been rejecting their hopes of marrying her.

Why would I want to get married? she asked herself. *So I can be as overworked and underloved as my mamm is?* No, she'd much rather stay single. Besides, her mother needed help raising the five boys. If Eliza hadn't been trying to appease her stepfather, she never would have accepted an offer of courtship in the first place.

"I understand it might seem as if I think more highly of myself than of my suitors, but I truly believe Petrus would be better off with someone else. I couldn't agree to marry him simply because he wanted me to or because I'm almost twenty-four and it's expected of me." Eliza wanted to add, *Or because you want another* mann *in the* familye *to help you in the workshop.*

Uri made crates and pallets for local farmers to use for storing and transporting potatoes and other produce. Over the last few years, his business had become so successful that he'd had a difficult time keeping up with the demand. Eliza's mother had suggested he hire a couple of teenage boys to help him on the weekends, but Uri insisted that a family business should stay strictly within the family. The more orders he received, the more Uri pressured Eliza to get married.

"You still haven't said precisely *why* Petrus isn't a *gut* match for you."

Eliza stalled, trying to think of a convincing reason why she wouldn't want to marry Petrus, other than she had no interest in getting married at all. She didn't want to belittle Petrus, since she genuinely liked him as a friend. So she appealed to her stepfather's interests instead, and said, "It's not just that Petrus wouldn't be a *gut* match for me. He wouldn't be a *gut* match for our *familye.* You've indicated how much you'd like to have a son-in-law who could help you with the business, but Petrus's *daed* expects him to continue working on the dairy *bauerei* after he gets married."

"What about his older *bruder*?"

"He's moving to Minnesota, so he can help his wife's *daed* on the *bauerei* there."

Uri pulled on his long, white beard as he mulled over this information. Eliza's stepfather was sixteen years older than her mother, who was forty-six. She, too, was graying, which her daughter attributed to stress, rather than to genetics. Her mother's ashen appearance served as a visual reminder of how much Lior needed Eliza's help at home.

"If you didn't believe you were a *gut* match for Petrus, maybe it's best that you ended your courtship with him after all," Uri finally conceded and Eliza breathed a sigh of relief. Until he added, "Especially since I've recently been approached by someone else who is interested in courting you."

"*You've* been approached?" Eliza repeated, unable to keep the scorn from her voice. Any man who would ask her stepfather's permission to court her, instead of asking her directly, was no man she'd ever accept as a suitor.

"*Jah.* Initially, I told him *neh* because I thought you and Petrus were still courting. But since you've ended your relationship with him, you should consider accepting Willis Mullet as a suitor."

Willis Mullet? He's closer to Mamm's *age than to mine!* The tall, overweight man had been a widow for eight years. He'd lived with his mother, who'd helped him raise his three sons, now eleven, ten and nine, until she died last winter. While Eliza could appreciate why he urgently wanted to remarry, she was alarmed to discover he was interested in courting *her.* Panicking, Eliza blurted out, "Willis is way too old for me."

"He might provide the maturity you need from a suitor. Besides, he's only thirty-six. That's thirteen years' difference between your ages. There's sixteen years separating your *mamm* and me."

That was exactly Eliza's point; she didn't want to follow in her mother's footsteps and marry an older man.

She didn't want to marry *any* man. Or *court* any man. Especially not one who seemed as dull and needy as Willis Mullet. But since her stepfather wouldn't be satisfied unless she was walking out with someone, she figured the least she should be allowed to do was choose a suitor for herself. "I—I know, but… But lately another *mann* has been paying special attention to me and I—I think he's on the brink of asking to be my suitor."

Uri raised an eyebrow. "*What* young *mann*?"

Lior again tried to intercede. "Maybe she'd rather not say, Uri."

But he persisted. "Is it the Yoder *bu*?" he asked and Eliza shook her head. "One of the Kanagy *breider*?"

Eliza nodded. Two Sundays ago after church, Freeman Kanagy had offered to give her a ride home. And in New Hope, when a man invited a woman to ride in his buggy, it was almost always either because he was courting her or he *wanted* to court her. Thankfully, Eliza had had the perfect excuse to turn him down; two of her brothers had gotten sick to their stomachs during lunch, so she'd had to dash home to help her mother get them bathed and into bed. However, Eliza was relatively certain that with a little playful banter, she could encourage Freeman to offer her a ride again this Sunday.

Her stepfather looked skeptical. "Don't the Kanagy *breider* own a *blohbier bauerei*?"

Eliza realized Uri was worried that if she eventually married Freeman, he wouldn't want to abandon the blueberry farm that he and his brother Jonas owned and come work with Uri. Of course, she had no intention of ever marrying Freeman, but since she couldn't tell her stepfather that, she addressed his concern, as she reminded him, "*Jah*, but that's not their main vocation—it's only a seasonal occupation. They both work as independent carpenters."

Her stepfather slowly nodded. Eliza could almost hear him thinking that a carpenter would be the perfect match for *him* as a business owner. Granted, Willis Mullet was employed by an *Englisch* construction company and he undoubtedly would welcome the opportunity to earn a living by working within the Amish community instead. But Freeman was much younger than Willis, so Uri probably assumed that meant he'd be more compliant with Uri's way of doing things.

"Okay. If the Kanagy *bu* asks to walk out with you before Willis does, I'll respect your decision. Otherwise, I expect *you* to honor *my* request and accept Willis as your suitor…at least for a few months."

Eliza stole a glance at her mother for support. But Lior was nervously eyeing the pot of water boiling atop the gas stove. They both knew they had to get back to work in order to finish everything there was to do before taking a day of rest on the Sabbath tomorrow.

Walking out with Freeman is better than walking out with Willis, she mused, rationalizing. *And it's definitely better than working away from home full-time, which would mean leaving* Mamm *alone during the day.* Her other consolation was that blueberry season was only a week or two away, so hopefully Freeman would be too tired to take her out very often. Or at least, not until later in the summer, and maybe by then, Willis Mullet would be interested in someone else.

"*Jah*, okay," she agreed.

But even before Uri had pushed back his chair and

stood, Eliza was silently praying something she never thought she'd pray. *Please, Lord, please, please, please let Freeman ask to be my suitor.*

Jonas Kanagy couldn't sleep. Right before he'd gone to his room, his brother Freeman had informed him that he was taking his own buggy to church the next morning instead of accompanying Jonas in his. *That confirms it,* he thought, brooding. *Freeman intends to give Eliza Keim a ride home. He wants privacy so he can ask to be her suitor.*

When the district members had met together for worship services two weeks ago, Freeman had announced he'd wanted to travel alone to church then, too. Jonas hadn't needed to ask him why: it was implicitly understood that when a young man or woman didn't ride with their family to or from church and didn't offer an explanation, it was because they intended to ride with one of their peers, usually of the opposite gender.

Not that Jonas would have questioned his brother, anyway—Freeman was twenty-three and he was free to go where he pleased. Besides, Jonas considered courting to be a private matter. But that didn't mean he wasn't deeply troubled by the likelihood that his younger brother was about to make a huge mistake.

He kicked off his sheet and flopped over in bed, thinking about the conversation he'd heard between Freeman and Eliza two weeks ago. Jonas hadn't meant to eavesdrop; he just happened to come around the corner of the church building at the same time Freeman offered Eliza a ride home.

"Maybe we can stop by Little Loon Lake on the way," his brother had suggested.

"*Denki* for asking, but I need to help my *mamm* with my *breider*. Peter and Samuel got sick after lunch and Mark looks a little green, too," Eliza had replied. Then she'd darted across the lawn and blithely called over her shoulder, "I hope you enjoy this beautiful weather!"

Jonas had managed to shrink back from view, so his brother hadn't known he'd overheard their brief conversation. Freeman had returned home a few minutes after Jonas and he'd been unusually quiet for the rest of the afternoon. But by Monday morning, he'd gotten his spring back in his step, and ever since then, he'd been whistling almost nonstop. Jonas suspected the cheerful tunes were a reflection of how hopeful Freeman felt about offering Eliza a ride home again this Sunday.

It wasn't surprising that he'd want to walk out with her. On the surface, Eliza was outgoing, gracious and quick to help whomever needed it. The way she interacted with her little brothers showed she possessed a lot of patience, as well as a good sense of humor. She was also unusually pretty, with chestnut-colored hair and amber-colored eyes, a heart-shaped face and very fair, flawless skin. So Freeman wasn't the only young man in New Hope who'd hoped to become her suitor.

Jonas knew this for a fact, because his closest friend, Petrus Kramer, had recently confided he'd courted Eliza for almost a year. According to him, the pair had never had a single argument during their courtship and Eliza had always seemed pleased to be walking out with him. So Petrus had felt blindsided when he'd brought up the topic of marriage and she'd responded by calling off their courtship altogether.

"I wasn't trying to pressure her—I told her I'd wait as long as it took until she was ready, but there was no convincing her," Petrus had said, bewildered. "I don't understand why just *talking* about marriage made her decide to break up with me."

Jonas didn't understand it himself. But he had an inkling of what was going on because he'd heard a rumor about something similar happening to another young man who'd once been Eliza's suitor. "It seems as if she's playing a game of some sort," he'd suggested.

"A game? What's her objective?"

"Who knows? But take it from me, it's better to find out sooner rather than later that she apparently didn't have any intention of marrying you."

Jonas knew that from personal experience. When he was twenty, he'd courted a woman from his home district in Kansas for eight months before learning she'd only entered into the relationship to make her previous suitor envious. Although she'd apologized profusely for her behavior and Jonas had forgiven her—he'd even attended her wedding—the experience had left him with a deep sense of distrust.

Four years later, he'd finally gathered the courage to ask to court another woman from his home district. He'd been her suitor for almost a year before she confessed she didn't care for Jonas the way he cared for her. She said she'd come to realize she'd primarily been walking out with him because her younger sisters were already married and she'd been worried she'd be a spinster forever. Although she hadn't deliberately meant to deceive Jonas, he'd felt tricked all the same. As well as hurt, angry and foolish. He decided the only way to guarantee that he wouldn't be used by a woman a third time was not to enter into a courtship again, period.

As it was, bachelorhood suited him just fine. It had been just two years since he and his brother had moved to Maine from Kansas. But he already liked it so much, and at twenty-seven he could imagine himself living alone here on the blueberry farm until he was old and gray, the way his uncle had done before him.

But Freeman has always wanted to get married and have six or eight kinner, Jonas thought. His brother had intended to get married when he was twenty, but the woman he loved had died unexpectedly from a congenital heart condition. Freeman had been absolutely despondent for a full year afterward. Then he and Jonas moved to Maine, and slowly the change of location and focus helped his brother recover emotionally from his loss. As far as Jonas knew, this was the first time Freeman was considering courting again.

After everything he's been through, I can't allow Eliza to break his heart the way she broke Petrus's, Jonas thought. But how could he stop her from doing that? He didn't want to tell his brother he'd overheard his conversation with Eliza two weeks ago. Nor could Jonas betray Petrus's trust by sharing what his friend had told him. Besides, even if he did, Freeman was very headstrong and he might not heed his warning.

If only someone else would become her suitor before my bruder *gets a chance to ask her to court her*, Jonas thought wistfully. *If I had any interest in a romantic relationship, I'd do it myself.*

All of a sudden, he sat up in bed. Actually, that wasn't a bad idea! The fact that Jonas had no desire to get married actually made him the perfect suitor for Eliza, because she couldn't possibly hurt his feelings by breaking up with him, no matter how long they courted.

Freeman would be disappointed, of course, but not nearly as crushed as he'd be if he walked out with her and then she broke up with him a year from now. Petrus was in Fort Fairfield for the summer, tending to his injured brother-in-law's farm. So Jonas figured his friend wouldn't find out about the courtship and feel as if Jonas had been disloyal to him.

Hopefully, before the summer ended, Freeman would set his sights on another young woman and forget all about Eliza. *Then I can call off our courtship without so much as a backward glance, just like she did with Petrus. Maybe a dose of her own medicine is the cure she needs to stop toying with* menner's *feelings...*

Of course, there was no telling if Eliza would accept Jonas as her suitor. Since he'd moved to Maine, he'd been on several outings with his single peers, including her. While she'd never exactly flirted with him, she'd always given him a winsome smile whenever they'd chatted. And she'd seemed genuinely interested in knowing how he was adjusting to Maine and what it was like to live in Kansas. *She may have just been acting hospitable and trying to make me feel* wilkom, he realized. *But since this the only plan I've got, it's worth a try.*

So the next morning, Jonas rose earlier than usual in order to take extra time making sure he smelled fresh, scrubbing his fingernails clean and shaving his face closely. When he was done, he lingered in front of the mirror, squinting his gray-green eyes as he examined both sides of his broad cheeks and jaw. He wiped a dab of shaving cream from one of the dark brown curls sticking out near his ear. Then he adjusted his suspenders evenly on his sturdy shoulders. There. That would have to do. Jonas donned his Sunday hat, said goodbye to his brother and went out the door.

In New Hope, as in the other Amish communities in Maine, every other week the district members met in an actual church building, instead of in each other's homes the way the Amish did in most states. The building had large windows, but there was no breeze circulating through the room. The weather was so warm that Jonas was perspiring by the end of the first hymn. By the time the three-hour service was over, his hair was limp against his forehead and his back felt slippery with sweat.

If Eliza sees the damp marks on my shirt, she's going to think I'm nervous about offering her a ride, Jonas thought. Which he was, in a way, but that was mostly because his brother's happiness was at stake.

After he'd eaten the community lunch, Jonas wandered outside with the other men. But instead of heading toward the hitching rail, he dawdled near the staircase so he could intercept Eliza as soon as she came out of the building. Jonas noticed that Freeman was across the yard, loitering beneath a maple tree. No doubt, he was trying to appear as if he was enjoying a moment in the shade, but his brother knew he was waiting for Eliza to come out of the church, too. Since he didn't want Freeman to see him, Jonas ducked around the corner of the building.

To his surprise, he discovered Eliza dallying there, almost as if she was waiting for someone. Or hiding.

She started, seemingly as surprised to see him as he was to see her. "Hello, Jonas. How are you?"

"Hello, Eliza. I'm *gut,* but hot." He nervously tugged at his shirt collar, regretting that he hadn't planned exactly what he was going to say to her. "How are you?"

"I'm *gut*, too. But you're right, it's awfully steamy out today. I'm not looking forward to having my five *breider* climb all over me like little puppies in the back of our buggy."

Jonas broke into a smile; this might be easier than he'd expected. "Would you like a ride home in mine instead?"

"*Your* buggy?" she repeated, as if the idea was unthinkable.

Jonas wished he could take it back but he swallowed and uttered, *"Jah."*

Before Eliza could say anything else, Willis Mullet popped around the corner. He greeted the pair of them and then said, "Your *daed* has been looking everywhere for you, Eliza. He said your *mamm* needed to get your *breider* home for their naps, but they couldn't find you. I told him to go ahead and leave—I'd be *hallich* to give you a ride home. My *seh* are going to the Stutzman *familye's haus* for the afternoon."

Jonas caught his breath. *Is Willis interested in courting Eliza? That could work out even better for me, as well as for Freeman*, he thought. But Willis was much older than Eliza, so maybe he was only offering her a ride as a friendly favor to her father?

"*Denki*, Willis," she said sweetly, and Jonas's heart

sank. Then she added, "But Jonas already offered me a ride, so I'm going with him."

Jonas's relief was short-lived because at that very second, his brother came jogging around the corner. He stopped short and his jaw dropped; there was no question he'd overheard what Eliza had said.

Freeman looked so crestfallen that Jonas was tempted to tell her he'd changed his mind and that she should ride with Willis instead. But that would have been rude. Besides, if it turned out that Willis wasn't interested in becoming her suitor—or if he was, but she said no— then there'd be nothing stopping Freeman from asking Eliza to walk out the next time he saw her.

No. Like it or not—and he didn't—Jonas was going to have to carry through with his plan.

Chapter Two

❧

Eliza's heart was drumming in her ears like hoofbeats, so she was grateful that Jonas didn't say anything as the horse pulled his buggy down the church lane and onto the main road. She needed a moment to make sense of what had just transpired.

Less than ten minutes ago, she'd been helping the other women wash and put away the lunch dishes in the church's basement kitchen when Honor Bawell, one of the older singles in the district, had sidled up to her. "A certain *mann* is looking for you in the gathering room, Eliza," she'd whispered gleefully. Honor relished being involved in matchmaking. "I told him if I found you, I'd send you upstairs to see him."

Assuming Honor was referring to Freeman, Eliza was relieved; if he was bold enough to make it known he was looking for her, then that meant he wanted to speak to her about something important. Namely, courting. But since Eliza hadn't wanted Honor to know she'd been expecting Freeman to seek her out, she'd played dumb, and nonchalantly asked, "A certain man? Who is it, my step-*daed*?"

"*Neh*, but he's almost old enough to be." Honor had tittered. "It's Willis Mullet."

Eliza had lost her grip on the platter she'd been rinsing and it fell into the soapy water, splashing suds on both of them. "*Denki* for letting me know," she'd said, but she hadn't budged from in front of the sink.

"I'll finish washing the rest of these so you can go talk to him," Honor had insisted, nudging Eliza out of the way with her hip. "He said he'll waiting near your *familye's* buggy, because he doesn't want to miss seeing you before you leave."

So instead of going up the main staircase to the gathering room, Eliza had escaped through the back basement exit. She'd crept around to the side of the building, with the intention of staying out of sight until she spotted Freeman Kanagy.

Before she'd left for church that morning, she'd spent fifteen minutes in front of the mirror practicing fluttering her lashes and twisting her prayer *kapp* ribbons around her finger, the way she'd seen some of her peers do when they were speaking with a man. That kind of flirting didn't come naturally to her, but she was so desperate to encourage Freeman to offer her a ride home that she was willing to use any trick she could.

However, when Honor had mentioned Willis was looking for her, Eliza's desperation intensified into full-blown panic. She would have preferred accepting a ride home on a motorcycle with an *Englischer* rather than going with him. So when Jonas discovered her lurking near the side of the building and offered her a ride home, she'd gladly accepted.

But now, seated beside him, she wondered how she could have misinterpreted Freeman's offer from two weeks ago. She supposed he could have asked to bring her home because he'd wanted to assess her interest in his brother, instead of in him. *I've heard that some menner are so shy, they ask a friend or bruder to speak to a weibsmensch on their behalf before they have enough courage to propose courtship directly to her*, she thought.

Jonas had never struck her as being bashful at all; in fact, they'd spoken several times, and if anything, he'd come across as more indifferent than shy. Not that he was arrogant, exactly, but that he'd never seemed to hang on her every word, the way some of her previous suitors had done prior to asking to court her. *Maybe the reason he wanted Freeman to get a sense of my interest has nothing to do with his being shy or saving face. Maybe that's just the custom in his home district in Kansas.*

Not that it mattered one way or another to Eliza whether she was courting Freeman or Jonas or any other bachelor in the district. All that mattered to her was that she didn't have to accept Willis as her suitor, as she'd promised Uri she would. *But if I don't think of a way to break the ice with Jonas, we'll be home before he gets the chance to ask me to walk out with him*, she realized.

Since he had to concentrate on guiding the horse along the road, it didn't make sense for Eliza to tip her head and bat her lashes the way she'd intended to do with Freeman. Instead, she tried to make her voice sound as coquettish as possible when she said, "It's so nice to have a chance to chat with you alone, Jonas. *Denki* for giving me a ride."

"You're *wilkom*."

His reply was so terse that Eliza wondered if she'd been reading too much in to his offer to bring her home, just as she'd misinterpreted his brother's overture. Or was Jonas simply nervous?

After a few more minutes of silence, she tried to draw him into conversation again, using one of the lines she'd rehearsed to say to Freeman. "I've actually been thinking about you a lot lately." Then she giggled, hoping to make it seem as if she'd unintentionally misspoken. "I mean, I've been thinking about your *blohbier bauerei*. It must almost be time for picking to begin?"

"*Jah*. We expect to open to the public a week from tomorrow."

"I'll be the first in line. All of my little *breider* love *blohbiere*. They love *blohbier* jam, *blohbier* pie, *blohbier* cobbler. They love *blohbiere* on ice cream and on cereal. I think they'd eat *blohbiere* on top of *blohbiere* if we'd let them."

Eliza laughed nervously. She realized she was rambling, but they were nearing the lane she lived on and she was becoming more and more fearful that Jonas wasn't going to ask to be her suitor after all. The thought briefly ran through her mind that if he didn't, maybe she could tell Uri that Jonas had given her a ride home and her stepfather would automatically assume that meant they were courting now. Then he'd back off about her considering Willis Mullet as a suitor.

Neh, Uri would never make an assumption like

that—he's going to question me directly and I can't lie about it, she silently conceded.

As Jonas drew the horse to a stop at the end of her lane, she said, "So, anyway, you'll be seeing a lot of me on the *bauerei* this summer..." She let her sentence hang in the air. She'd done her best to set the tone for talking about courtship, but now it was up to him. As she waited for a response, Eliza actually did twirl her prayer *kapp* ribbon around her finger, but it was anxiety, not coyness, that made her fiddle with it.

Jonas shifted in his seat to face her. Sweat was dribbling down both sides of his face, but his mouth must have been dry because he licked his lips. In all of the times she'd spoken to him, Eliza had never really noticed how full his mouth was. Or that his upper lip formed such a perfect bow—it looked as if it had been stitched that way. It was a strange thing for her to notice now, but perhaps that was because she was so apprehensive about what he'd say next that she couldn't stop staring at his mouth.

"I think you'll find the *biere* are unusually sweet this season. They might not be quite as plump as last year's, but Freeman and I think the flavor is going to be more concentrated. Not quite as sweet as wild *blohbiere*, but still, very *gut*."

This wasn't the kind of sweet talk Eliza had hoped she'd hear from Jonas and she was losing heart. But she replied, "We can pick lowbush *biere* up the hill, right behind our barn. Oddly, my *breider* prefer the cultivated kind."

She told him the story about how the previous year, her mother had served the last of the berries to four of her brothers over ice cream as a special afternoon treat. The youngest boy, Mark, found out about it when he woke up from his nap, so naturally he wanted the dessert, too. Since they were all out of the cultivated berries, Eliza had sneaked up the hill to pick some of the smaller wild berries as a substitution. But when Mark saw them, he'd pushed away the bowl and said he didn't want baby berries, he'd wanted the grown-up kind.

Once again, Eliza recognized she was blathering, but she couldn't seem to make herself get out of the buggy without a courtship proposal. Thankfully, her anecdote seemed to put Jonas at ease. He chuckled and said, "I'd never even seen wild *blohbiere* until I moved to Maine, so I can understand your *bruder's* disappointment in being served the littler *biere*."

"Really? There aren't any wild *blohbiere* in Kansas?"

"*Neh*. It can even be difficult to grow the cultivated kind there, especially in the western part of the state. But we do grow lots of sunflowers. Fields and fields of them, taller than you and nearly as bright as, well, as the sun." Jonas rubbed his chin, a faraway look in his eyes. "I guess that's why Kansas is nicknamed the sunflower state."

"I didn't realize that. I've never been out of the pine tree state, so I always enjoy hearing you talk about Kansas." Eliza was being so sincere that she momentarily forgot about her mission to get Jonas to ask her to walk out with him. So she was surprised by the way he responded.

"I—I always enjoyed talking to you, too, Eliza. And actually, I'd like—I'd like to get to know you better," he said. She studied his expression, still unsure if he meant what she hoped he meant. Beads of sweat trickled down both sides of his face and he wicked them away with his palms before sweeping off his hat. His hair was plastered to his head and it seemed as if the poor man was melting before her eyes. But the gesture was so polite it made Eliza feel guilty that he was clearly trying to make a good impression on her. "I—I mean, I'd like to court you."

"That's *wunderbaar*!" she exclaimed. In her exuberance, she grasped his forearm. She released it just as quickly and drew back, trying to compose herself. No matter how relieved she was that he wanted to be her suitor, she couldn't allow Jonas to believe a courtship meant they were on a path to marriage. "I'd really like to get to know you better, too, Jonas. Although, I have to be very candid about something…"

As he cocked his head to the side and narrowed his eyes, a few droplets of sweat spattered from his hair onto his shoulder. "What's that?"

"I—I'd like our courtship to progress slowly. I want us to become better friends first. Without any expectation or pressure that…" She didn't even want to use the word *marriage*, so she said, "That we'll develop a closer relationship in the future."

She could barely meet his eyes. After flirting so blatantly with him, Eliza couldn't help but wonder if he felt as if she'd pulled a bait and switch. Was he going to rescind his offer of courtship now that she'd told him she essentially wanted to keep their relationship platonic?

Jonas had to bite his tongue so he wouldn't chuckle out loud. Partly, his urge to laugh was because he was relieved that Eliza had agreed to walk out with him. And partly it was because he was amused that she wanted their courtship to progress slowly. Jonas couldn't have hoped for a better response if he'd scripted it himself.

"I completely understand. We can develop our relationship as slowly as you'd like—you can set the pace," he told her. "In fact, with everything there is to do on the *blohbier bauerei,* I probably won't be able to walk out with you during the next few weeks. I'll be working until dusk every weekday evening and all day on *Samschdaag,* too."

"That's *wunderbaar,*" Eliza exclaimed for the second time, before quickly explaining herself. "I mean, it's *wunderbaar* that you don't mind taking time to develop our friendship. And I have no expectation for us to walk out in the evenings, especially during *blohbier* season. I'll see you in *kurrich* and on the *bauerei,* which will be nice. But I know that being out in the sun all day can sap a person of his energy, so I understand if you're just too worn out to socialize afterward."

"*Gut,* it's agreed, then." Jonas realized he sounded as if he'd just confirmed a contract for a carpentry project for one of his *Englisch* customers. "I—I mean, I'm *hallich* we both understand one another's preferences and I look forward to courting you."

That sounded just as stiff, but Eliza didn't seem to mind; she was absolutely beaming. Jonas had to give her credit; the other two women he'd courted weren't nearly as easygoing about his schedule. They'd expected him to take them out every Saturday evening and for a buggy ride or picnic after church on Sunday, too.

"I'll hop out here," she said, indicating she didn't

want him to pull all the way up the lane to her house. "Otherwise, my *breider* will see us and ask me a hundred questions about why I got a ride home from you instead of joining them in my *familye's* buggy. I'd like to keep our—our courtship as private as we can."

Jonas couldn't help but notice the word *courtship* seemed to stick in her throat. But maybe he was just imagining that because the word felt so strange to his own ears. Twenty-four hours ago, if someone had told him he'd be courting Eliza Keim—or anyone else—he would have checked the sky for flying pigs.

Yet now, as he rode home, he happily mused, *That was easier than I ever dreamed it would be. The way Eliza was flirting with me, it almost seemed as if she was as eager for me to become her suitor as I was to get her to walk out with me.* Then again, maybe Eliza would have been equally flirtatious with *any*one who'd offered her a ride home. Maybe that was part of whatever game she'd played with her previous suitors?

For someone who'd nearly bounced out of her seat when he asked to court her, she made a big point of emphasizing she wanted their courtship to progress slowly. Come to think of it, maybe she'd been *too* agreeable when he'd claimed he wouldn't be able to take her out very often this summer.

Suddenly, it occurred to Jonas that maybe she was toying with him, playing a game of cat and mouse. Perhaps that was what happened with Petrus and her other suitors, too… Perhaps she'd drawn closer and then distanced herself from them throughout their courtships, right up until the point when they'd wanted to discuss marrying her. But why would she do that? It seemed rather cruel.

I really shouldn't speculate, Jonas reminded himself. *Even if she behaves the same way toward me as her other suitors, I won't be affected by it, because I'm not going to get emotionally involved with her.*

As far as he was concerned, the more distance Eliza wanted to put between them and the slower she wanted their relationship to develop, the better. In fact, he wouldn't mind if they didn't spend any time alone together until *blohbier* season was over at the end of August. And by then, it might not be necessary to take her out, because Freeman might ask someone else to court him.

Jonas pulled up the long, gravelly road leading to the house and farm. His happiness about how well things had turned out with Eliza was bittersweet, since he knew that the worst part of his whole scheme—facing his brother—was yet to come.

After unhitching the buggy and cooling down his horse, he meandered across the driveway. *Pretty soon, we'll have people coming and going in and out of here all day.* This would be his and Freeman's third summer running the "U-pick" blueberry farm they'd inherited from their uncle, and Jonas felt as excited about opening day now as he'd felt about it the first year they'd been here.

While he enjoyed the work he did as an independent carpenter—building decks, installing cabinets and laying floors—there was something about being outdoors all day tending to God's creation that Jonas liked just as much. Not that the work was that laborious. Although the men had to take care of pruning, irrigation, and disease and insect control, their uncle had done all the hardest work of planting and cultivating. By the time the Kanagy brothers inherited the land, the shrubs were fully productive.

The only improvement they'd made to the farm was to turn it into a U-pick operation. This not only saved them the time and effort of harvesting the fruit themselves, and the expense of hiring someone else to do it, but it also meant they didn't have to pay to have the fruit transported to nearby markets, since their horses could only travel so far in a day.

Their farm was very family-friendly, and *Englischers* and Amish customers alike frequently brought their children with them to pick. The *Englisch* families especially enjoyed that Jonas or Freeman gave them rides in the horse-drawn flatbed "buggy wagon" to the barrens farthest from the parking area. The brothers employed a young Amish woman, Emily Heiser, to weigh the fruit, run the cash register and assist the customers as needed, but they didn't have any other employees. All in all, the Kanagy brothers' farm was a simple but satisfying business, and Jonas was grateful his uncle had bequeathed it to them, even though they missed their family and friends back in Kansas.

I should encourage Freeman to leave the bauerei *early on* Friedaag *and* Samschdaag *evenings so he can socialize with his peers*, Jonas thought. *It will give him the chance to become better acquainted with the young* weibsleit *in our district, now that he's ready to court again.*

As he neared the house, he spotted his brother relaxing in a glider on the porch. Freeman had changed out of his church clothes and was sipping homemade root beer that they'd bought in a big jug from Millers' Restaurant, which was owned by a local Amish family. "You're back sooner than I expected," he said when Jonas climbed the steps and sat down. "I thought you would have stopped off at Little Loon Lake on your way home."

"Why would I have done that?" Jonas asked, feigning ignorance. He needed to make absolutely sure Freeman was aware that he and Eliza were courting.

"Because I overheard you offering Eliza a ride in your buggy. She enjoys canoeing on the lake, so I figured you might have taken her there."

Little Loon Lake was accessible from a public parking lot at the town beach, but the Amish people in New Hope could also access it through the Hilty family's backyard. The district members had chipped in to purchase two canoes and a rowboat for the community's use. They stored the canoes, which could be used on a first-come, first-serve basis, in the Hiltys' shed near the water. Jonas had gone fishing on the lake several times and he'd enjoyed it, but he hadn't known Eliza liked canoeing, too. It made him feel a little guilty to realize his brother must have thoughtfully planned to take her there when he'd offered her a ride two Sundays ago.

"*Neh.* I just took her straight to her *haus.*"

"Then you didn't ask to court her?"

Jonas didn't have to pretend to be chagrined. Even though he expected Freeman's question, he was genuinely embarrassed to be talking with his brother about courting. Or maybe it was the shame of knowing he was being deceptive that caused Jonas's cheeks to burn. "That's—that's kind of a personal question."

"I promise I won't tell anyone at all. I just really need to know."

"*You* need to know? Why?" Jonas asked, although he could guess Freeman's answer.

"Because if you aren't courting her, I'm going to ask her to walk out with me. It's been over three years since…" Freeman's voice faltered, and as he took another sip of root beer, Jonas looked out over the lawn so he wouldn't have to see the flicker of emotion darken his brother's expression. But he recovered quickly and started over. "It's been three years since Sarah passed away and I feel ready to court again. I've spoken to Eliza several times and I think highly of her."

Freeman's lingering sadness over Sarah's death confirmed for Jonas that he was doing the right thing by preventing his brother from getting hurt again. But he still felt terrible admitting what he'd done. "I—I actually *did* ask Eliza to court me."

"Did she say *jah*?"

He nodded, still unable to meet his brother's eyes.

To his surprise, Freeman chortled. "You look so miserable, I was sure she'd turned you down."

Surprised, Jonas glanced at him. "You're not disappointed that I asked her to walk out with me?"

"Actually, I'm glad you beat me to it. If she said *jah* to you, obviously you're the one she's interested in. So you spared me the humility of being rejected face-to-face." Freeman's mouth curved into a self-conscious smile. "I actually kind of wondered if there was someone else she wanted to court or if she was already courting. I offered her a ride home two weeks ago and she turned me down. She said she had to help take care of her sick *breider*. I couldn't quite tell if she was being genuine or if she was just making an excuse to spare my feelings. It's been so long since I've courted that I feel like I don't trust my intuition about *weibsmensch*."

Freeman's good-natured concession made Jonas feel even worse about the situation. "I'm *hallich* you feel ready to start courting again. Some *weibsmensch* is going to be very blessed to have you as her suitor. In fact, I was just thinking that if you want to spend more time socializing, you don't need to stick around the *bauerei* until closing time on the weekends. I can manage on my own."

"What about Eliza? She's going to expect you to take her out."

"*Neh*, she won't. I already explained to her that I'll have a lot to do on the *bauerei* and I probably won't get to see her too often until *blohbier* season is over."

Freeman's eyes widened. "You told her that? What did she say?"

"She completely understood."

His brother lifted his hat and rubbed his forehead as if he had a headache. "Wow, and I thought *I* was out of practice as a suitor... Listen, Jonas, you can't ask to court a *weibsmensch* and then tell her you don't have time to see her for a couple of months. She might have indicated she was fine with that arrangement, but trust me, she isn't. Or even if she is right now, it won't last very long. The entire point of a courtship is getting to know each other, and you can't do that if you don't spend time together."

But she said she wanted to take our courtship slowly, Jonas thought. Aloud, he argued, "I've known several long-distance courtships that have resulted in marriages. And those couples spent very little time with each other because they lived so far apart."

"They may have lived far apart, but you can believe they were writing letters almost every day. Or spending lots of time at the phone shanty calling each other." Freeman swallowed the last of his root beer. "Trust me, if you don't take Eliza out at least once a week, your courtship will be over before it begins... And if that happens, don't blame me if I make a second attempt to court her myself!"

Even though he was sure—or almost sure—that his brother was joking about becoming Eliza's suitor if she broke up with him, Jonas didn't find Freeman's remark to be one bit funny.

I'm actually going to have to treat this arrangement more like it's a real courtship after all.

The realization was so nerve-racking that if Jonas hadn't already been perspiring for hours, he would have broken out in a cold sweat.

Chapter Three

"Your *mamm* and I noticed you stayed in your room last evening," Uri said to Eliza a week after Jonas asked to court her. Since it was an off-Sunday, they'd just finished holding their home worship service. The boys had been dismissed to play outside and Eliza was edging out of the living room toward the kitchen so she could help her mother prepare a light lunch.

"*Jah*, that's right, I did." She explained that she'd been working on knotting an oversize rag rug that she'd hoped to take to Harnish Hardware Store on Monday morning for consignment. However, she'd gotten too tired and hadn't been able to finish it before going to bed. Since today was the Sabbath and the rugs were a source of income, she couldn't work on it this afternoon, either.

Uri thrummed his fingers against his knee, the telltale sign he was impatient or displeased, but Eliza couldn't figure out why. She thought he'd be happy she was trying to earn more money to contribute to their household expenses. "Are you going out this afternoon?" he asked her.

"I don't know." Her friend Mary Nussbaum sometimes stopped by on Sunday afternoons. On occasion, if her two youngest brothers were napping, Eliza would accompany Mary to Little Loon Lake, where the two women would go canoeing. But if all of the boys were awake, Eliza preferred to stick close to home, so she could help her mother keep an eye on them. "Why do you ask? Do you and *Mamm* need me to watch the *buwe* at home so you can go pay someone a visit by yourselves?"

"*Neh*. I wanted to know if the Kanagy *bu* was coming to take you out since you said he asked to be your suitor," Uri replied, referring to Jonas as "the Kanagy boy" because he couldn't remember either of the brothers' names, she was sure.

"Jonas *did* ask to be my suitor." Eliza struggled to keep any hint of defensiveness out of her voice. Firstly, because Uri had almost made it sound as if she'd been making up the fact that she and Jonas were courting. And, secondly, because it wasn't any of his business how many times a week they went out. But since she knew that wouldn't stop her stepfather from questioning her further, Eliza provided the explanation he was seeking. "He's been busy preparing to get the *blohbier bauerei* ready. Opening day is tomorrow."

Uri made a disgruntled sound. "He can't work on a farm after dark, nor can he work on it on the *Sabbaat*."

Aware he was implying that Jonas should have been available to take her out in the evenings or on the weekend, Eliza said, "I don't mind. I appreciate that he's such a hard worker."

"A young *mann* should show more interest in the *weibsmensch* he's courting," Uri grumbled, almost as if *he* was the one who felt slighted by Jonas's inattentiveness. "He might not be a *gut* match for you, either. I believe you would have been better off with Willis Mullet."

Please, Gott, *help me not to respond in anger,* Eliza silently prayed before she spoke. "Jonas has only been my suitor for a week. It will take time for *me* to discover whether he's a *gut* match or not." Emphasizing the word *me* was as close as she dared come to telling Uri he didn't have any say in the matter. Eliza excused herself and went into the kitchen to help her mother make peanut-butter-and-strawberry-jam sandwiches for the boys, and ham-and-cheese sandwiches for the adults.

"Did I hear you say tomorrow is opening day for the *blohbier bauerei*?" Lior asked her. "I don't know where my mind is—I'd completely forgotten."

"*Jah.* I plan to go picking at around nine or ten o'clock. I can take the three older *buwe* with me, so they can help me pick."

"Wouldn't you rather go by yourself so you can talk to Jonas without your *bruder* interrupting?"

"*Mamm*, you sound just like Uri, trying to rush my courtship," Eliza complained. "I wish neither of you knew Jonas asked to be my suitor."

An injured look crossed Lior's face. "My intention wasn't to interfere in your courtship, Eliza. I only want you to feel free to socialize without always having to take care of your *breider*."

Eliza regretted hurting her mother's feelings. She wished she hadn't reacted so strongly, especially since it was really Uri's meddlesomeness she found so exasperating, not her mother's. "*Denki*, I appreciate that you were trying to be helpful, *Mamm*. But I honestly didn't intend to go to the *bauerei* to socialize with Jonas. I want to pick *blohbiere* so we can get started making jam, as well as all the other treats the *buwe* like so much. Besides, Jonas is going to be too busy to stand around chatting with me."

"Oh, he might be busy, but any suitor worth consideration will go out of his way to spend time with the *weibsmensch* he's courting, even if it means working twice as hard when she's not around."

Lior's comment was almost exactly the same as what Uri had said, but this time Eliza didn't take offense because she noticed the dreamy expression on her mother's face. She assumed Lior was thinking about being young and courting Eliza's father. Henry Keim had died when Eliza was six. Since she hardly had any memories of him, she loved hearing her mother reminisce about what he was like or tell her stories about things he'd done.

"When you and *Daed* were courting, did he always take time to chat with you, even if he was busy?" she asked.

"*Jah*. And so did Uri. I remember when he spent an entire afternoon taking me on errands because our *gaul* had thrown a shoe and the farrier was in Canada visiting relatives. It was your twelfth birthday and the weather was bitterly cold. I decided to walk into town because I needed to pick up the winter boots I'd ordered for your present, as well as purchase cocoa so I could make your favorite chocolate-buttercream frosting for the birthday cake. I'd just recovered from the flu and Uri didn't think I should be walking so far in that kind of weather. He insisted it wasn't a problem for him to take me into town. I didn't find out until much later that he'd had a big order to fill for a customer by the next morning, so he'd worked until midnight to make up for the lost time."

"I didn't know he did that," Eliza said. Although the anecdote was admittedly sweet, she was disappointed that her mother had told a story about Uri instead of her father.

"*Jah*, he did a lot of thoughtful things like that when we were courting."

It's too bad he doesn't still *do thoughtful things like that for you*, Eliza thought. *But once you married him, he probably figured he didn't have to try so hard to win your affection anymore.* That was another reason she had no intention of getting married—she doubted most men could sustain the romantic, thoughtful gestures they practiced when they were courting.

"Lior!" Uri called from the other room. "I'm *hungerich*. Is lunch almost ready?"

"*Jah*, it's all set." Lior turned to her daughter. "Could you please go round up the *buwe*?"

Eliza hurried outside and circled the house, where she spotted the boys at the bottom of the small hill in the backyard. "Mark, Eli, Samuel, Isaiah, Peter! Time for lunch!" she called. All of them except Samuel charged past her to go inside. The six-year-old had just rolled down the hill and he must have still been dizzy because he only took a few cautious, crooked steps like a newborn foal before falling onto his bottom. Eliza had to stifle a giggle as she went over to help him up again. As they walked, she held his sweaty palm to keep him steady.

"*Denki*, 'Liza. The ground is tipping," he said.

"The ground isn't tipping—*you* are. It's called being dizzy," she explained. "I'm surprised you don't have a *bauchweh*, too."

"*Neh,* my *bauch* is empty, so it doesn't hurt. What did you and *Mamm* make for lunch?"

"*Aebier*-jam-and-peanut-butter sandwiches. I know those aren't your favorite, but guess what?"

"What?"

"Tomorrow I'm going *blohbier* picking, so pretty soon we'll have *blohbier* jam and peanut butter sandwiches, instead of *aebier*. You can *kumme* with us and help me pick this year. I think you're tall enough now."

"I can? Wait until I tell the other *buwe*." Samuel dropped Eliza's hand and started to run. He staggered for a few steps and she thought he would take another tumble, but he quickly straightened out and made it to the porch without falling.

Watching him, she couldn't help but smile. Although her little brothers were a handful, they were also a delight. *They're one of the few reasons I'm glad* Mamm *married Uri,* she thought.

After Eliza's father, Henry, had died in a tree-falling accident, Eliza and Lior had moved back in with Lior's parents. Lior's father had passed away two years after that, and her mother perished within months of him. So Eliza and Lior had lived by themselves from the time Eliza was nine until she was thirteen. The two were very close, and in some ways, they felt more like sisters than mother and daughter. As far as Eliza was concerned, they could have happily lived alone like that forever.

Lior's parents had left her a small house and their modest savings. Times were tight, but it wasn't as if Eliza's mother urgently needed to get married for financial reasons. But Eliza supposed she must have been desperate for adult company—that seemed the only logical reason she would have ever courted someone like Uri. And he'd clearly fooled her into thinking that he'd be as kind and considerate a husband as he'd supposedly been as a suitor.

Not that he was ever really *mean...* But in Eliza's eyes, he was never really pleasant, either. Although she felt guilty for thinking it, sometimes it seemed to Eliza that her stepfather had always resented how close she and her mother were. *That's probably one more reason he's so eager to marry me off and get me out of the* haus. *He'd rather have* Mamm *all to himself, even if it means she'll have no one here to help her with the* buwe.

Well, he could pressure Eliza until the cows came home, but there was no way she was ever going to get married. And *pretending* to court was as close as she was ever going to come to actually courting.

But considering how closely Uri is monitoring this courtship, I'm afraid I'm going to have to do a better job of pretending. And I can't do that unless Jonas starts showing more interest in me.

It was only ten o'clock on Monday morning and the parking area near the barn was already almost filled with *Englisch* vehicles. Jonas realized he was going to have to set out orange cones and rope off a section of the yard to indicate additional spaces the customers could use. While he was thrilled that the business was off to such a great start, he felt a little overwhelmed.

Despite their best preparations, Jonas and Freeman had suffered an unexpected setback yesterday. After they'd worshipped together and eaten lunch, Jonas had announced he was going to the phone shanty to call his family in Kansas at two o'clock, the way he usually did on off-Sundays.

"When you're done talking to *Mamm*, are you going to pick up Eliza and take her canoeing or on a picnic?" Freeman had asked.

"Whether I am or not, it's none of your concern," Jonas had replied. Even though he'd had no intention of going anywhere with Eliza, he didn't want Freeman to know that. "I hope you're not going to be checking up on me throughout my courtship, because I won't appreciate it."

"Okay, okay, I'll back off. I just want to make sure Eliza doesn't feel ignored, that's all."

Jonas would much rather have gone hiking in the gorge with Freeman and other singles from their district, but if he had done that, his brother definitely would have known that Jonas hadn't gone out with Eliza. Of course, there'd been the possibility that *she* might have shown up for the hike by herself, but there was nothing Jonas could have done about that.

When he'd arrived at the phone shanty, he'd discovered a message on the voice-mail system from Emily, the young woman Jonas and Freeman had hired to work the cash register on the farm. She'd said she was visiting relatives in Serenity Ridge and her return trip to New Hope was going to be delayed because her mother had the flu and was too sick to travel. Emily had said she wouldn't be able to come to work until Tuesday or Wednesday morning.

So, because they were short-staffed, opening day at the farm was a little more hectic than usual. Freeman had to stay at the cash register booth so he could weigh the fruit and collect money from the customers. Jonas, meanwhile, had been trying to manage the daily chores and upkeep of the barrens in between giving customers rides to and from the parking lot in the buggy wagon. He'd quickly realized that transporting *Englischers* such a short distance wasn't a good use of his time, and decided they'd just have to walk, the way the Amish people did.

However, half a dozen customers complained that their children had been waiting all year to ride in the buggy wagon because it was such a novelty to them. Some *Englischers* even hinted that the horse-drawn ride was the reason they patronized the Kanagy brothers' farm, instead of the U-pick farms closer to where they lived. So Jonas resumed shuttling them back and forth, and he even took an extra lap around the perimeter of the farm just for fun as a way of retaining customer satisfaction.

But now, he was ready to switch responsibilities with Freeman for an hour. As he neared the cash-register booth, Jonas noticed his brother was talking to an Amish woman who had several small children with her. He was approaching them from behind, so at first he couldn't tell who it was, but when he got a little closer he recognized Eliza and her little brothers.

"Do you *menner* want your own baskets, or are you going to put the *blohbiere* you pick in your *schweschder's* basket?" Freeman asked the boys.

"Our own," the two tallest ones replied in unison, so Freeman handed them each a wooden basket that had a length of rope looped through the handle for tying the container around their waists.

"How about you?" Jonas's brother crouched down to speak to the smallest boy. "Do you want your own basket to put your *blohbiere* in, too?"

"Neh," he said seriously, shaking his head. "I'm not going to put mine in a bucket. I'm going to put them in my *moul*."

Freeman and Eliza cracked up together. Then Freeman teased, "In that case, you'd better hop up on this scale so I can weigh you. Then, when you're done picking, I'll weigh you again."

"Why?"

"So I know how much to charge you for all the *blohbiere* you ate."

Once again, Eliza laughed. Actually, she cracked up harder than Jonas would have expected her to. It wasn't *that* funny, at least not to Jonas, who had heard his brother make a variation of that same joke several times before now. He cleared his throat and stepped forward, interrupting their chatter. "Hello, Eliza."

She glanced up from helping one of the boys tie the basket around his waist. "Oh, hello, Jonas. It looks as if you're having a very successful opening day so far."

"*Jah*. There are a lot more customers than we expected."

"They probably want to get a head start on perfecting their recipes for the *blohbier* festival."

The *Englischers* in New Hope hosted a blueberry festival the second weekend in August. Held on the town's fairgrounds, the festival was an opportunity for farmers, bakers and vendors to sell blueberries by the pint, as well as blueberry jams and desserts. Nonedible items for sale included blueberry-scented candles, hand towels embroidered with blueberries, photographs of local blueberry barrens and other decorative household knickknacks. The festival also offered various activities and events, live music performances, a road race and, of course, a blueberry-pie-making contest—which was followed by a blueberry-pie-*eating* contest.

It would have been considered *hochmut* for Amish women to enter the baking competition, but several of them chipped in to share a rented space at the festival so they could market their blueberry confections and other handiwork.

"Are you participating in the festival, Eliza?" Freeman asked.

"*Neh*. My *bruder* love *blohbiere* so much that we have to use every *bier* we pick for jams or treats for our *familye*. There's never anything left over for us to sell."

"What about the rugs you make—don't those have *blohbiere* on them?"

Jonas thought, *I wasn't aware she made rugs for sale—how is it Freeman knew that about her?* It concerned him that his brother was so familiar with Eliza's preferences and hobbies.

"*Neh*. They're rag rugs, not embroidered," she answered. "In order for me to be able to sell them at the festival, they're supposed to be related to *blohbier* season."

"Aren't any of them the color *bloh*?" Freeman joked.

Eliza smiled. "*Jah*, but I don't think that counts. You'd be surprised by how seriously the festival organizers are about these things. Last year they closed down the stall next to ours because the vendors were selling *aebier* jam, if you can believe it."

Freeman's eyes got big. "You're kidding, aren't you?"

When Eliza giggled, Jonas decided he'd better do something to interrupt their banter a second time, so he told his brother it was his turn to shuttle the customers between the parking lot and the barrens.

"Sure," Freeman said good-naturedly. "I'll wait to give Eliza and her *breider* a ride, too. They've walked all the way from her *haus* so they're probably hot and tired."

Jonas didn't want to appear rude by suggesting his brother should leave without her, but he really wanted to speak to Eliza by himself. Given the way Freeman was kidding around with her, Jonas was starting to feel nervous that she might decide she preferred his brother's company to Jonas's. *I've got to arrange to spend time with her alone very soon*, he thought. But how could he do that if Freeman whisked her away?

Thankfully, Eliza said, "That's okay, there's no need to wait, Freeman. The more worn out my *breider* are, the less likely they are to wander away and get lost in the *blohbier* bushes. Besides, I think I need a longer rope for my basket. This one doesn't go all the way around my waist."

"That's because that one is for a *kind's* basket. Just a second—I'll find you an adult-size piece," Jonas offered. But first, he turned to his brother and pointedly dismissed him. "See you later, Freeman."

After Freeman had left and Jonas retrieved a longer piece of rope for Eliza, he was still at a loss for how he was going to manage to set a date with her in front of her little brothers. He could tell they were antsy to start picking berries and he knew he had to think quickly, but his mind drew a blank.

"Oh, *neh*, I'm all thumbs," Eliza said, reaching around behind her back. "I tied my basket on too tight, but I think it's in a knot, so I can't loosen it. Could you please help me with it, Jonas?"

She's been tying an apron around her waist every day since she was a maedel—*certainly she should be able to work a knot out on her own by now*, he thought. But then it occurred to Jonas that she was *flirting* with him. Once again, she'd presented him with a better solution for his dilemma than he could have ever thought of on his own.

"Sure, I'll give it a try," he said. As he loosened the knot, he was close enough to lean forward and whisper in her ear. "I'm sorry I didn't get to see you yesterday, but may I take you for a ride next *Sunndaag* after *kurrich*?"

"I'd like that a lot," she whispered back, turning her head ever so slightly. Her face was so close to his that if they'd actually been courting and no one else had been around them, he might have been tempted to kiss her cheek.

The unbidden thought was so disquieting to him that Jonas stepped back and said to her brothers, "If your teeth are *bloh* when you *kumme* back, I'll know what you've been eating!"

When Eliza laughed just as hard at his joke as she'd laughed at Freeman's, Jonas breathed a sigh of relief. He didn't have anything to worry about…at least, not until next Sunday, when he had to take Eliza out for the first real date of their fake courtship.

Chapter Four

"Stay on the grass, *buwe*, or else you'll have to *kumme* back here to hold my hand and walk with me!" Eliza called for a second time to three of her brothers, Peter, Isaiah and Samuel. It was Thursday morning and the boys were gallivanting up ahead of her and Mary on their way to the Kanagy brothers' blueberry farm. Even though the quiet country road had a wide, gravelly shoulder, Eliza felt they couldn't be cautious enough around *Englisch* traffic. The boys obeyed and moved farther to the left, onto the grassy field. To Mary, she said, "Sometimes I feel like I'm herding goats."

Mary chuckled. "Don't you mean sheep?"

"*Neh.* It would be much easier to herd sheep."

"I wish I had little *breider* to herd." Mary was the youngest of seven daughters, all of whom lived out of state. So she didn't even get to see her little nieces and nephews very often. "Better yet, I wish I had *kinner* of my own." Unlike Eliza, she'd occasionally indicated that she was eager to get married and start a family, but she'd never had a suitor.

"One day soon, you will. But this morning, I'm *hallich* you're here to give me a hand with my *breider*. When we went picking on *Muundaag*, Peter got stung by a bee and Isaiah accidentally spilled all of the *blohbiere* out of his basket when he bent over to pick up a snake."

Mary stopped short in her tracks as if she'd just seen a reptile herself. "You saw a snake in the *blohbier* barrens?"

"I didn't—Isaiah did. It was only a green snake. They hardly ever bite."

"Even so, their slithering bothers me." Mary shuddered and then resumed her pace beside Eliza. "Do you suppose you can *kumme* canoeing with me and a few others from *kurrich* this *Sunndaag*? Honor is getting a group together. I think Keith, Glenda and Ervin intend to go."

"I, um, I wish I could, but I can't." This Sunday after church, Eliza's mother, brothers and Uri were going kite flying with a few other couples who had young children. So it would have been an ideal time for Eliza to accompany her friend—if only she hadn't already committed to going for a buggy ride with Jonas.

"Oh, that's too bad. Do you have to watch your *breider* again?"

"*Neh*. I..." Eliza hesitated. Mary was her closest confidante besides her mother, so she'd told her about each of the suitors she'd had in the past. Although she hadn't confided the *reason* she'd agreed to be courted by them, she'd let Mary know when she was courting and when her courtships had ended. But after having five suitors in as many years, she felt a little self-conscious admitting to Mary that she was courting a sixth, when her friend hadn't ever courted anyone at all.

However, Mary guessed the reason for Eliza's pause. "Don't tell me—you have another suitor, don't you? And you've already made plans with him for *Sunndaag*."

Eliza nodded and replied in a low tone so her brothers wouldn't hear. "*Jah*. He asked to be my suitor about two weeks ago, but we haven't gone out anywhere together yet. So he's taking me for a buggy ride after *kurrich*."

"I see." Mary pressed her lips together, and for a while, the only sound between the two young women was the crunching of the gravel beneath their sandals as they strode toward the farm. Eliza glanced at her friend's profile and recognized the disappointed expression on her face.

"Please don't be upset." Eliza assumed Mary felt let down that she couldn't go canoeing with her. "I know I've only been able to go to the lake with you once this summer, but unfortunately, I have to honor the first commitment I made."

"Unfortunately?" Mary repeated incredulously. "If you feel it's unfortunate that you're going to spend time with your suitor, why did you agree to walk out with him in the first place?"

Eliza quickly backtracked, and stammered, "I—I didn't mean it's *unfortunate* I'm spending time with him. I meant it's unfortunate that I already made a commitment to him because I'd prefer to go canoeing with you and everyone else on *Sunndaag*." Her explanation did little to appease Mary, who seemed uncharacteristically expressive this morning.

"I don't understand you, Eliza. You're my closest friend and I'm *hallich* that you appreciate the *schpass* we have together… But if the shoe were on the other foot, I'd rather go out with my new suitor than spend *Sunndaag* canoeing with you and the other singles," she admitted.

"Thanks a lot," Eliza said drolly.

"All I mean is that it's perfectly natural for a *weibsmensch* to be excited about going out alone with her new suitor. But you seem to act as if it's a dreaded chore," Mary said. "Maybe that's because when a person has had as many suitors as you've had, courting loses its shine."

"You're making me sound like an *Englischer* who dates someone different every couple of months," Eliza protested. "I haven't had *that* many suitors."

"You've had a lot more suitors than I've ever had— although I guess that wouldn't be difficult to do." Mary whisked her fingers over her cheek and Eliza couldn't tell if she was brushing away a tear or shooing a fly. "I hoped to be married and have a *kind* by now. I never thought I'd get to be this age without ever even having a suitor. It makes me wonder if *Gott's* will is for me to be single the rest of my life."

"Don't be *lappich*. You're only twenty-two."

"My *schweschdere* were married by the time they were twenty-one and they'd all had their first *bobbel* within a year."

"It isn't a race," Eliza reminded her, even though she understood why Mary might feel as if it was. "You shouldn't feel pressured to get married just because other *weibsleit* our age are married."

"I don't feel pressured. I feel *envious*," Mary confessed. "I know I should be content with my life, whether I'm single or married. But I truly hope it's *Gott's* will for me to fall in love, get married and become a wife and a mother—and the sooner, the better."

Even though Mary had sometimes mentioned that she wished she'd had a suitor and she'd occasionally commented that she couldn't wait to become a mother, she'd never spoken about it as openly and with such longing as she did today. Although Eliza didn't want to get married herself, she wanted her friend to have the deep desire of her heart. "If that's what you really want, then I'll pray the Lord will allow it to happen," she offered.

"Denki." Mary was quiet for a moment, then ask, "Now, are you going to tell me who your suitor is?"

Knowing she could trust her to not tell anyone else, Eliza said, "Jonas Kanagy."

"Really?"

"Why do you sound so surprised?"

"Well, it's just that…" Mary stopped to shake gravel from her sandal, then replied, "To be frank, Honor mentioned that Willis Mullet was looking for you after *kurrich* the other week. She had the notion he was going to ask you to walk out with him. But you know what she's like—anytime a *mann* and a *weibsmensch* so much as glance at each other, she assumes they're courting."

Eliza didn't bother to acknowledge that in this instance, Honor was more right than wrong about Willis's intentions. *"Neh*, it's Jonas who's courting me."

"Oh." Mary gave a funny little laugh. "I actually thought his *bruder*, Freeman, might be interested in you. At the risk of sounding like Honor, the few times when he has stopped to chat with us after *kurrich* lately, I've noticed how attentive he always is to everything you say."

Although Eliza had thought the same thing at one point, she now realized she'd made the wrong assumption, too. "He's just a *gut* listener."

"Mmm-hmm. If you say so," Mary teased.

"What does that mean?"

"It means I wish *menner* would fawn all over me the way they fawn all over you."

"Don't be *narrish. Menner* would fawn all over you if they had the chance to get to know you better. I've grown up with the *buwe* in our district, but you're a relative newcomer to Maine."

"A newcomer? I moved here six years ago! The *menner* in our peer group have had plenty of chances to get to know me better. If they really wanted to, they would have done it by now."

Eliza had to weigh her words carefully before she replied, since she didn't want to hurt her friend's feelings. Mary was a warm, thoughtful, lovely person, but when she was around men, she had a tendency to withdraw. During their outings with their male peers, she was so reserved that at times she almost seemed disinterested. Additionally, she was very pretty, with ash-blond hair and big blue eyes that appeared even larger when she wore her silver-framed glasses. Eliza suspected that the men their age felt somewhat intimidated about approaching her, so they mostly kept their distance.

"Maybe—maybe they just need a little encouragement," she tentatively suggested.

"You think I should *flirt* with them?" Mary said the word *flirt* as if the idea was completely appalling to her. Eliza wasn't sure that was because Mary came from a very conservative background or because she simply found flirting to be too disingenuous for her personality. It was probably a little of both.

"*Neh*, not necessarily. But sometimes *menner* don't know how to get a conversation started or they lack the confidence to speak with a *weibsmensch* one-on-one. If you initiated a conversation with one of them, it might put him at ease." Up ahead, Eliza's brothers were turning onto the dirt driveway, heading for the booth to collect baskets to put their berries in. She called out, reminding them to keep an eye out for *Englisch* vehicles. Then she asked Mary, "Is there any *mann* in particular you'd consider accepting as a suitor?"

"I—I guess so," she admitted, her cheeks going pink. Her voice dropped even lower as she said, "Lately I've noticed that Freeman has been attending more social events. There's something about him that seems kind of, well, different from most of the other *menner* our age. But like I said, he only seems to have eyes for you—at least, that's what I thought."

Eliza snapped her fingers. "I have an idea. I'll suggest to Jonas that we should go canoeing, too. You, Freeman, Jonas and I can all ride together to the lake on *Sunndaag* after *kurrich*." Not only would riding there together give Eliza the opportunity to facilitate a conversation between Freeman and Mary, but it would also prevent the conversation from becoming too personal between Eliza and Jonas. The longer she could keep their discussions on a superficial level, the better.

"But how are you going to get Freeman to agree to go, too?"

They were within a stone's throw from the booth where Emily Heiser was tying a blueberry bucket around Samuel's waist. Eliza answered Mary in a whisper. "Just leave it to me. I'll think of something."

"Look who's here." Freeman elbowed his brother. It was almost lunchtime and they were returning from the northern-most section of barrens, where Jonas had been showing Freeman that the birds had been feasting on blueberries.

"*Jah,* I see her," Jonas replied noncommittally. He'd noticed when Eliza, her brothers and Mary Nussbaum had arrived earlier that morning, but he hadn't sought out Eliza to talk to her for several reasons. Firstly, he was too busy. Secondly, he didn't want to show her any special attention in front of Mary, since he didn't want Mary—or anyone else—to suspect that they were supposedly courting. Thirdly, and most importantly, Jonas was at a loss for trivial topics to discuss with Eliza; he actually hoped to "save" his small talk for when he took her for a buggy ride on Sunday.

However, there was no avoiding chatting with her now because she had spotted him and Freeman, and was lifting her hand in a wave. The littlest of the three boys, Samuel, also waved and smiled a blue-toothed smile. Jonas couldn't help but chuckle.

The Kanagy brothers headed toward the booth, where the group was clustered around the scale. Everyone exchanged greetings as Emily weighed their berries and carefully poured them into the buckets Emily and Mary had brought to transport the fruit home.

"Looks like you picked enough to make several pies," Freeman commented to Eliza. "If your *breider* here are tired of eating *blohbiere,* feel free to bring any leftover pie to Jonas and me. It's my favorite."

Eliza answered, "My *blohbiere* are for making jam, not pie. But Mary's baking pies and they're always *appenditlich*. It's a *gut* thing for the *Englisch* that she can't enter them in the contest at the *blohbier* festival, because she would win, hands down."

"*Neh*, there's nothing special about my pies," Mary said modestly, shaking her head as she looked down at her shoes.

"I'd be happy to be the judge of that," Freeman offered with a laugh. "And when I'm done eating, I can tie the empty pie tin to a post to frighten away the birds."

"Oh, *neh*. Have they been eating the *biere*?" Eliza asked.

"*Jah*. They've helped themselves to that entire area over there." Jonas waved his hand to indicate the northern section of the farm. Then he turned to Eliza's brothers and asked, "Can you guess what kind of bird has been eating the *blobhiere*?"

Isaiah shrugged and Peter shook his head, but little Samuel took a guess. "The *hungerich* kind?"

Jonas, Freeman, Eliza and even quiet Mary burst out laughing. "That's a better punchline than what I was going to say," Jonas admitted.

"What kind of birds were you going to tell us ate the *blohbiere*?" Eliza asked.

"Why, bluebirds, of course," Jonas replied with a

friendly smirk and she chuckled at his joke. "Although I think the bluebirds had some help from their friends, the robins and starlings. The damage is pretty widespread."

"That's a shame." Once again, Eliza sounded very empathetic. "If it would be helpful, I could make a scarecrow for you?"

"*Denki*, but there's no need to go to that trouble," Jonas said, declining her offer, although he was grateful for it. "We'll pick up some scare tape at Harnish Hardware Store."

"What's scare tape?" Samuel asked, wide-eyed, as if he were imagining something very frightening.

"It's a kind of shiny ribbon that we can fasten to the *blohbier* bushes," Jonas explained. "Kind of like the tinsel that *Englischers* decorate the *Grischtdaag* tree with in the center of town. The ribbon reflects the sunlight, and when the wind blows, it dances around and makes a crinkling sound, which the birds don't like. So it keeps them away from our *blohbier* bushes."

As Jonas was talking, he noticed two *Englisch* women and about half a dozen children gathering around the buggy wagon near the other side of the parking lot, apparently waiting for a ride out to the barrens. So he suggested to Freeman, "Looks like you've got customers waiting for you. And I should get back to work, too."

Freeman started walking toward them, then called over his shoulder, "Don't forget—if you need anyone to eat leftover baked goods, I'm up for the job. It doesn't have to be pies, either. I also like *blohbier* muffins and *blohbier* crumble."

Jonas ruefully shook his head at his brother's blatant

hinting, but Eliza just giggled. "We'll remember that, won't we, Mary?" she said.

Mary didn't seem as amused as Eliza was. Ignoring the question, she said, "It's almost lunchtime. We should be getting back or your *breider* will get so *hungerich* they'll eat half the *blohbiere* before we make it to your *haus*."

"Okay. But I was just going to ask Jonas if I could have a glass of water before we leave. The *buwe* guzzled down the entire jug we brought and I'm so thirsty." She looked directly into his eyes and Jonas could tell she wanted to discuss something in private with him. He dared to hope she was going to tell him she had to cancel her plans with him on Sunday after all.

"Sure. Do you need a drink, too, Mary?" he asked, but she said she'd brought her own thermal bottle of water, so she had plenty to drink. So Jonas led Eliza toward his house, careful to keep at least three feet of distance between them so no one—Amish or *Englisch*—would suspect they were a couple.

"I always thought the *buwe* walked quickly, but I can hardly keep up with you," Eliza said when they'd gotten halfway across the lawn, so he slowed his pace a little, but not so much that they could easily make small talk.

"I'll be right out," he told her when they reached the porch. He took the steps two at a time, then dashed into the house and back out a moment later with a tall glass of water, which he extended to her.

"Denki."

As Eliza tipped her head upward and slowly drained the glass, her reddish-brown hair glinted with sunlight. For a second, Jonas pictured her shiny locks loosened from the bun she wore at the nape of her neck and blowing in the breeze. Quickly looking away, he dismissed the image as something that had simply popped into his head because they'd just been discussing reflective scare tape.

After she handed the glass back to him, he set it on the bench where he and Freeman had left their root-beer glasses the previous evening. "I'd better get going," he remarked, hastily hopping down the stairs.

"Wait, just one second, please." Eliza hurried down the stairs, too. Shielding her eyes, she looked up at him. "I was wondering if you had a particular destination in mind for our buggy ride on *Sunndaag*?"

Jonas's thought about how pretty Eliza's hair was had left him feeling so unsettled that he'd completely forgotten she must have had an ulterior motive for asking for a drink of water. Without thinking, he answered bluntly, "*Neh*, not yet. But I will." Once the words were out of his mouth and Eliza discovered he hadn't put any consideration into planning a special outing for them, Jonas expected her to scowl or frown. Instead, she smiled.

"Actually, since you don't have specific plans yet, I was wondering if we could go canoeing at Little Loon Lake," she suggested. "Honor is getting a bunch of people together and I thought it would be *schpass* if we joined them."

Jonas couldn't believe it. For what must have been the third or fourth time, Eliza was providing him with an easy road out of his predicament. "Sure. If that's what you'd prefer to do instead of going for a ride, I'd enjoy it, too." *Socializing with a group of people will be a lot more* schpass *than spending the afternoon pretending to be romantically interested.*

"Wunderbaar." She smiled and added, "I know Mary would like to go, too. If she rides with us, people won't suspect that you and I are courting."

Jonas just *knew* there had to be a catch. "I, um, well..." he stuttered. It wasn't that he minded giving Mary a ride, too, but showing up to a group event with two women just wasn't something a typical Amish man in this district did. At least, not unless one of the women was his sister. It seemed to him that Eliza should have known it wasn't a custom here, too. But since she apparently didn't see why he might think it was inappropriate, he said as tactfully as he could, "I'd feel kind of outnumbered by *weibsleit.*"

"Oh, *jah.* You're right, I can see what you mean." She nodded in agreement and took a few steps, but then stopped and held a finger in the air. "I have an idea. If Freeman doesn't already have other plans, maybe he could *kumme* with us, too? No one would give it a second thought if the four of us traveled there together."

Even though she was acting as if the thought had just occurred to her, there was something about Eliza's solution that just seemed a little *too* convenient, as if she'd had it in mind all along. Was he imagining it, or was it possible that Eliza was becoming more interested in keeping Freeman's company than in keeping Jonas's? She certainly seemed to enjoy talking to Freeman and kidding around with him. But then again, Eliza was generally a very amiable person and she'd laughed at Jonas's corny jokes, too, so maybe he was misreading the situation.

Still, he was tempted to tell her that he'd changed his mind about going to the lake after all. But he'd already agreed to it and if he broke his word, he might lose her favor altogether. So he did the only thing he could. "Sure, I'll ask him if he wants to *kumme*."

"Great. I'll let Mary know I mentioned the outing at the lake to you and that you and your *bruder* are going and you agreed to give us a ride. We'll meet you at your buggy after *kurrich*."

That wasn't exactly how the conversation had gone, but Jonas said, "Sounds *gut*. See you then." As he strode off, he thought he heard Eliza say something else, but he didn't catch it because he was silently praying that Freeman had already made plans to do something else on Sunday afternoon.

Chapter Five

"**W**on't you please *kumme* fly kites with us, too?" Samuel pleaded to Eliza as they rode to church on Sunday morning.

She shifted her youngest brother, Mark, to her other knee. At three years old, he was still just small enough that he had a difficult time staying seated on either of the narrow benches facing each other in the back of the buggy, so it was safer for her to keep him firmly in her arms. Rather than tell Samuel she was going out with Jonas, Eliza replied, "If I *kumme*, there won't be enough kites for everyone."

"That's okay. I'll share mine with you. *Mamm* says *Gott* likes it when we share with a cheerful heart."

Eliza smiled at the dear little boy; she should have known not to give him such a feeble excuse. "*Denki.* That's very generous of you. Next time we have a breezy *Sunndaag,* maybe I'll be able to join you. But today I'm going canoeing with my friends."

"Your friends?" he asked. "Mary?"

"*Jah*, she'll be there," Eliza answered.

At the same time, Lior gently scolded him from the front of the carriage. "Samuel, that's none of your business."

Generally speaking, it was considered impolite for Amish children to question adults about their plans. However, Eliza found her six-year-old brother's curiosity more understandable and less intrusive than her stepfather's, who asked, "What do you mean, Mary will be there? I thought you were going out—"

Eliza noticed her mother tap Uri's shoulder and raise her finger to her lips. So Uri was quiet a moment before he rephrased his question in a way the boys wouldn't understand. "I thought you were going out with your other...*friend*."

"*Jah*. I am. There is a group of us going," Eliza cryptically assured him even though she resented the infringement on her privacy. She'd told him earlier in the week that she and Jonas were spending Sunday afternoon together. That was already more information than Eliza felt she should have had to share. Couldn't he just leave it at that?

She silently asked the Lord to give her patience and to take away her resentful feelings, but she still felt annoyed all the way to church. Those feelings lingered throughout the worship service as well. She felt like canceling her plans with Jonas just to prove to Uri that he wasn't in control of her social life. But that was just it: Uri *was* in control of her social life, at least to the extent that he insisted Eliza should have a serious suitor.

Besides, she really was looking forward to canoeing, and she was committed to helping Mary get to know Freeman better. Her friend, however, had expressed second thoughts about going when Eliza told her about the arrangement she'd made with Jonas to invite his brother.

"Oh, *neh*!" she'd cried. "I didn't realize you were going to speak to Jonas about it directly. He probably thinks *I* put you up to matchmaking. If Freeman finds out, he'll think I'm being very forward. Now he's going to avoid talking to me altogether."

"Don't worry. I made it seem as if I was the one who wanted you to *kumme* along so no one would know Jonas and I are courting. He and Freeman won't suspect a thing. When it comes to courting and romance, *menner* can be completely oblivious about a *weibsmensch's* interests," Eliza had said. She should know; she'd been tricking her stepfather about *her* interest—that is, her lack of interest—in suitors for over five years.

Thinking about it now, as the minister read a passage from the third chapter of Colossians that included a verse about not lying to one another, Eliza felt a little twinge of shame. Not about matchmaking for Freeman and Mary, but about purposely misleading Uri. But she quickly dismissed her qualms, rationalizing that her stepfather was so controlling that he left her with no other choice. Besides, it wasn't as if she'd been outright lying to him—or to her mother—anyway.

Nor have I been lying to my suitors, she silently justified. *I've always been very straightforward about not necessarily wanting anything more than an opportunity to develop friendships with them.*

Indeed, judging from the few interactions she'd had with Jonas so far, she believed she genuinely would enjoy becoming friends with him. Eliza liked the way he engaged with her brothers, and she appreciated how agreeable he was about going to the lake on Sunday, instead of for a ride. Also, her connection to him was already allowing her to help Mary get better acquainted with Freeman. *For all I know,* Gott *has allowed Jonas to be my suitor just for that very purpose*, she told herself.

Yet if that was true, then why did she still feel so relieved when the minister's sermon about truthfulness was finally over?

"You want to sit in the front with Eliza?" Freeman asked out of the corner of his mouth as Eliza and Mary approached Jonas's buggy after church.

"Neh," Jonas whispered urgently. "Remember, you have to pretend you don't know anything about us courting. That's the entire reason Eliza wanted you and Mary to *kumme* with us—she doesn't want anyone to know I'm her suitor, including *you.*"

"Hello!" Eliza called, and Mary echoed her greeting. They were each carrying an insulated half-gallon jug, which presumably contained water or lemonade for the group to share.

The brothers hardly had time to say hello back before Honor came dashing toward them from the opposite direction, a sizable cooler bag in hand. "Oh, *gut*—you haven't left yet," she said, panting. "I was going to ride with Glenda, Ervin and Keith, but Keith's *groossmammi* and *groossdaadi* arrived yesterday as a surprise for his *daed's* birthday. So he's staying home with them. I didn't want to ride alone with Glenda and Ervin because I'd feel like a third wheel, if you know what I mean."

She gave an exaggerated wink, which was unnecessary because everyone knew exactly what she'd meant.

"You're *wilkom* to join us," Jonas said. Eager to get on the way before Honor could catch her second wind and continue gossiping, he said, "I can hold your bag while you get in."

"*Denki*, Jonas. You're such a gentleman." Honor's syrupy tone made Jonas regret offering.

"And I can take those for you." Freeman held out his hand to take the jugs from Eliza and Mary, then joked, "I'm just as much of a gentleman as my *bruder* is."

Eliza laughed and handed over the bottle before climbing into the back of the carriage, but Mary held on to hers and stated, "It's only a half gallon of water. I think I can manage, *denki*."

On the way there, Honor talked so much that no one else got a word in edgewise. Not that Jonas minded; it was actually kind of a relief to have her do all of the talking because he was preoccupied with other thoughts.

Eliza certainly seems to be amused by Freeman, he mused. *Or does it just seem that way because Mary is so reticent by comparison?* In either case, to be on the safe side, he decided when they reached the lake, he'd try to keep as much distance between Freeman and Eliza as possible. But how could he separate the two of them in a way that wouldn't result in him winding up alone with Eliza?

Thankfully, an opportunity presented itself almost as soon as they arrived at the lake and met up with Glenda and Ervin. "Glenda's wrist is still healing from when she fell and sprained it last week, so she shouldn't paddle. I can take her in the rowboat. That means there will be three of you in one canoe and two in the other, okay?" Ervin suggested, making it clear he preferred to be alone with Glenda in the rowboat, even though it had room for three people.

"Sounds *gut*," Jonas agreed. "You and I can share a canoe, Freeman. The *weibsleit* can go in the other one together."

Freeman looked incredulously at his brother and opened his mouth, undoubtedly to object, but Honor beat him to it. "It's so rare for even one of you Kanagy *buwe* to *kumme* on an outing with us. How will we get to know you better if you only keep company with each other?"

"*Jah.* She's right. I talk to you morning, noon and night. It's time for us to chat with someone else," Freeman said to Jonas, smirking. "I'll take two of the *weibsleit* in my canoe and you can take one in yours."

Jonas knew Freeman was setting it up so that it wouldn't seem suspicious for Jonas to go alone in the canoe with Eliza, and for once, he didn't mind his brother's interference in his supposed courtship. However, before he could answer, Honor again piped up. "I'll go with Jonas. Mary and Eliza, you can go with Freeman."

Jonas shot his brother a pleading look but Freeman gave him a shrug as if to say "Sorry, but what can I do?"

Eliza said the arrangement was fine with her and hurried to put on a life vest. She seemed more eager than disappointed to be relegated to Freeman's canoe with Mary. *Is that because she doesn't want Honor or the others to figure out we're courting, or is it because she prefers Freeman's company to mine?* Jonas wondered, irritated that such thoughts were plaguing him.

"Let's head toward Pine Island," Ervin suggested a few minutes later as the three vessels shoved off from shore.

Pine Island was how they referred to the little clump of land in the middle of the lake. Surrounded by jagged rocks and densely populated with pine trees, the rectangular-shaped island was probably only seventy feet long and thirty feet wide, but it was a popular picnicking spot because it afforded a cool, shaded resting or fishing area in the middle of the lake.

"Okay," Jonas agreed, then pointedly added, "After we take a break there, we can switch paddling partners."

"Are you tired of me already?" Honor asked, sounding dejected. "We haven't even gotten our paddles wet yet."

Realizing he'd insulted her with his suggestion, Jonas joked, "*Neh*, but my *bruder's* arms will probably be tired so he'll want someone else to paddle by then."

"*Voll schpass,*" Freeman remarked from his canoe, where he was sitting in the back. Mary was in the middle and Eliza was paddling in front. "If my arms are so weak, why are we ahead of you?"

"You won't be for long," Jonas quipped. "We'll race you to the island, won't we, Honor?"

"*Jah.* Let's go!"

Jonas put all of his strength into paddling, and Honor was a strong, confident paddler herself. The pair quickly overtook and then outpaced Eliza, Mary and Freeman's canoe. Ervin and Glenda apparently decided not to race at all because when Jonas glanced over his shoulder, he noticed they were lagging so far behind that it was clearly intentional.

"We won!" Honor exclaimed when she and Jonas reached the shallow, rocky area surrounding Pine Island several minutes before anyone else did.

"*Gut* paddling," Jonas acknowledged. He navigated them around the boulders jutting up above the water and situated their canoe parallel with the embankment. He told Honor she should get out first, but when she stood she said she felt "too tippy" and promptly sat back down. So Jonas got out and dragged the boat about fifteen yards through shin-deep water to where there was a flat, sandy area, so Honor could easily step onto it. Regardless, as she stood up, she extended her hand to him. Reluctantly taking hold of it, Jonas thought, *She didn't have any difficulty balancing when she was getting* into *the canoe*. As soon as her second foot hit dry land, he released her fingers.

It wasn't that he disliked Honor, but he did recognize that she'd earned the reputation she'd developed for being rather bold in her behavior toward the bachelors in the New Hope district. He supposed it was understandable; Honor was one of the older single women and she clearly wanted to get married soon. But the community was small so she probably didn't have a lot of options for suitors. However, Jonas didn't want to do anything to encourage her to think *he* might be one of those options. *I'm not even interested in being* Eliza's *suitor... and I'm actually courting her*, he thought wryly.

So when Honor suggested Jonas should sit with her on a large log in the shade, he declined, making a joke at Freeman's expense to soften his refusal. "*Denki*, but I'd better not. I've got to stand here and make sure my *bruder* doesn't capsize his canoe on a rock."

Honor giggled. "Do you really think he might tip it over?"

"*Neh*, probably not," Jonas admitted. "But better safe than sorry."

Shading his eyes as he peered out over the water, he watched Freeman and Eliza paddling toward the island, with Glenda and Ervin's rowboat still far in the distance behind them. As Freeman's canoe came closer, Jonas could see Eliza was scowling. *Maybe she doesn't enjoy being with my* bruder *so much after all.* And although he wouldn't have deliberately *wished* a bad time on her, Jonas couldn't help but feel a little bit relieved.

This is not *how I envisioned spending the afternoon*, Eliza thought as she silently brooded. She was hot, sweaty and annoyed that Jonas had suggested racing across the lake. *How is Mary supposed to chat with Freeman when he's so intent on getting to the island? Honor and Jonas already won the race and Glenda and Ervin aren't even trying, so what's the big rush?*

Not that Mary could easily chat with him, anyway, since she deliberately sat facing forward instead of facing Freeman, but she could at least say something over her shoulder. Instead, Eliza's friend had been virtually silent for the entire excursion toward Pine Island. *How does she expect Freeman to be interested in her when she's acting as if she wouldn't give him the time of day?* Eliza wondered.

But what really had gotten her goat was that Jonas seemed to be showing Honor an inordinate amount of attention. Granted, there was little he could have done when Honor declared she was going to paddle in the same canoe with him. And Eliza figured he was just being polite by holding Honor's bag for her when she got into the buggy—after all, Freeman had done the same for her. But Eliza had distinctly spotted Jonas taking Honor's hand and helping her out of the canoe when they'd reached the island just a moment ago.

I know I said I didn't want anyone to find out we're courting, but that doesn't mean I want him to show special attention to Honor, she thought. *If he's not careful, she'll think he's interested in her.* It wasn't completely far-fetched for Eliza to imagine that Honor might tell her mother about her misperception, and that Honor's mother would be so delighted that she'd share the news with someone who'd share it with *Eliza's* mother. Or worse, that Uri would somehow hear the rumor.

I can't allow that to happen, Eliza thought. So when they approached the embankment and were ready to disembark from the canoe, she sweetly asked Jonas, who was standing close to the water's edge, "Could you take my hand, please? I feel shaky, probably from all that exertion."

Eliza was almost certain she heard Mary snicker behind her—after all, they'd both hopped in and out of the canoe easily without assistance countless times before. But there was too much at stake for her to care if her friend thought she was acting sappy. Jonas took her fingers in his, and she was surprised by the softness of his touch. After holding his hand a moment longer than necessary, so Honor would see them, Eliza finally let go.

But Honor was bending over her own canoe, fishing her cooler bag out of it, and she apparently hadn't even noticed. Eliza realized she'd forgotten the jug of iced tea she'd made for everyone to share in the canoe. "Oops," she said. "I forgot—"

"It's okay. I'll carry it. I know how dizzy you are," Mary said drolly. Then she hopped out of the canoe, a jug in each hand, without so much as a wobble.

"Wow, Mary. You have the balance of a cat," Freeman remarked as he clumsily hefted himself onto dry land.

Not exactly the most romantic compliment, but it's a start, Eliza thought, pleased. It seemed Mary was pleased, too, because even though she didn't respond aloud, a blush rose on her cheeks and forehead.

Once Glenda and Ervin had come ashore, the group climbed farther up the embankment to sit on an old fallen tree and on the numerous rocks or stumps in the area. Mary and Eliza distributed paper cups of water or iced tea to everyone, while Honor passed around a tin of blueberry muffins that she'd made. Everyone except Freeman refused the offer, saying they were still full from eating lunch at church.

"More for me," Freeman said gratefully. "I'm starving and I love any dessert made from *blohbiere.*"

How is it possible that Freeman has lived here for over two years and has attended dozens of kurrich *potlucks and yet he doesn't realize what a* baremlich *baker and cook Honor is*? Eliza wondered to herself. She wasn't being unkind: Honor's cooking was notorious in New Hope. In fact, it was even notorious in the surrounding communities of Serenity Ridge and Unity. To be sure, her lack of simple culinary skills was an anomaly among Amish women, much like it would have been for an Amish man to lack basic carpentry skills.

Yet even more unbelievable was the fact that she seemed oblivious to how bad the food she prepared actually tasted. Despite several frank comments from her mother and others in the community, Honor's enthusiasm for cooking and sharing the desserts and dishes she'd made never waned. So Eliza watched intently as Freeman took his first bite of a muffin.

Honor was also watching intently. "How is it?" she asked.

"Mmf," he mumbled, still chewing. He swallowed and then downed a big gulp of iced tea. "I've never tasted *blohbier* muffins quite like these."

Eliza recognized he was being as diplomatic as he could while still being truthful, and she momentarily felt bad for Honor, who really did try very hard. However, Honor appeared clueless as to what he really meant, and commented, "I'm *hallich* you like them. You and Jonas should take the rest home with you. Since you're bachelors, it's probably rare for you to eat homemade treats."

"*Neh*, that's okay," Freeman replied, a little too quickly, waving his hands for emphasis. "One is enough for me."

Honor quizzically wrinkled her brow. "But you just said you loved *blohbier* desserts."

Freeman avoided answering by taking another swallow of iced tea, so his brother chimed in, "*Denki*, Honor. That's very considerate of you."

She beamed at him and then someone brought up the subject of the blueberry festival. As everyone else was talking, Eliza mulled over Jonas's response to Eliza. It was clear to her that he was covering for his brother's impoliteness and she was impressed by this small kindness. She tried to catch his eye so she could smile at him, but he was gazing out at the lake. As she studied his profile, she found herself thinking, *For someone with such a prominent, masculine-looking jawline and forehead, he sure does have soft, pretty eyelashes...*

The seven of them must have relaxed on the island for a good hour, joking, telling stories about what they'd been doing over the summer and even singing a few contemporary worship songs together. Eventually, they made their way back down to the water and waded around the rocks for a while before Glenda said she had promised to be home before suppertime, so she needed to leave.

"I'll take you back," Ervin quickly volunteered before anyone else could lay claim to the rowboat.

"I need to head home, too," Mary said, to Eliza's dismay. Although no one would have considered her friend to be gabby, she'd certainly been engaging in the conversation more than she usually did when men were included. Eliza could tell she was having a good time and Eliza was enjoying herself, too. She'd forgotten how carefree she felt when she didn't have to keep an eye out for her little brothers.

"Okay. But I know how much you like to paddle and you haven't gotten a chance yet," she replied to Mary. "My arms are tired, so I'll sit in the middle of the other canoe with Jonas and Honor, as long as they're willing to do all the work." This seating arrangement seemed like the best of both worlds. It would give Mary the opportunity to visit with Freeman, while preventing Eliza from being alone with Jonas.

"Sure, I'll paddle," Honor agreed. "Jonas seems to steer us exactly in the direction I want him to go, without my even telling him to head left or right. We make a really *gut* team, don't we, Jonas?"

He shrugged. "You are a strong paddler, but for my part, there's not much I have to do to guide the canoe. It's pretty much a straight line from the Hiltys' beach to the island."

For some reason, Eliza felt bothered by his response. *I'm a strong paddler, too*, she thought, even though she knew it was prideful, regretting that she'd pretended her arms were tired. Which was odd, because it wasn't as if she had anything to prove to Jonas. "I hope you don't plan to race again," she remarked, knowing that if they raced, Mary wouldn't be able to enjoy a leisurely discussion with Freeman.

"Why not? You'll be on the winning team this time," Honor teased.

"Suit yourself, but you'll be paddling into the wind." She climbed into the canoe and sat with her back toward Jonas. There was no sense facing him since they weren't going to converse, anyway. *I know I asked him not to let anyone know we're courting, but he has spent more time chatting with Honor than with me. What if he's as interested in her as she apparently is in him?* she thought, worrying.

As they set out for the opposite shore, it occurred to her that while Honor may have won the previous race to the island, Eliza couldn't allow her to win over Jonas's affections. It wasn't that she wanted him to develop any romantic feelings toward *her*—after all, that was what had happened with Petrus and it had ended in him being bitterly disappointed. But she couldn't risk Jonas dropping her to court Honor.

If that happens, I'll be stuck walking out with Willis. So from now on, no more group outings—Jonas and I are going to go out alone, she resolutely decided.

Freeman and Mary easily won the race. Once both teams had crossed the lake and everyone had disembarked at the Hiltys' property, Glenda and Ervin had to leave right away. So the other three women put the paddles and life vests into the storage shed while Freeman and Jonas hoisted the canoes onto the storage rack.

As they were dragging the rowboat to drier ground, Freeman whispered, "On the way back, you can let me off at Abram's *haus*—I'll say I want to drop in and see if he's home. That way, you'll have some time alone with Eliza."

"*Neh*, I won't—she lives farther away from our *haus* than Honor does." Jonas intended to drop off the women according to the proximity of their houses from the lake. Which meant first he'd stop at Mary's house, then Eliza's and then Honor's.

"You still don't get it, do you?" Freeman muttered. "Anyone can tell by her expression that Eliza's annoyed at you. You've been paying more attention to Honor than to her this entire afternoon."

His comment really riled Jonas. Partly because he knew his brother was right. But mostly because Jonas felt like *Freeman* was paying even more attention to Eliza than Jonas had been paying to Honor. "What excuse will I give for dropping Honor off first and then circling all the way back to drop off Eliza? It will be obvious that I want to spend time alone with her, just like it's obvious that Ervin wants to be alone with Glenda. If you think Eliza seems upset with me now, how do you think she'll feel if Honor finds out I'm courting her?"

"*Jah*, I guess you're right." Freeman lifted his straw hat to wipe his brow. "But mark my words, Eliza is not *hallich* with you."

It's not my fault she wanted to go on a group outing, Jonas silently observed. Regardless, for his own sake, he couldn't allow their afternoon to end on a sour note. So when he stopped at the end of Eliza's lane, Jonas made a point to get out of the buggy and give her his hand to help her down, something he'd never ordinarily do if they were just friends. At least, not unless she cajoled him into it, the way Honor had done.

He was worried that Eliza would push away his arm or ignore him, but she slid her hand into his. Just as when he'd helped her out of canoe, he was aware of how slender and silky it felt. Instead of letting go when both of her feet touched the ground, he led her to the side of the buggy, out of Honor and Freeman's range of view, and then he released her fingers.

In a hushed tone, he said, "I had *schpass* at the lake today. But I think it would be nice if we went out alone next time, if you wouldn't mind?"

"*Neh*," she replied firmly and Jonas's stomach dropped. Was she really *that* annoyed at him? But in the next breath she clarified, "I wouldn't mind at all."

"*Wunderbaar*," he uttered in relief. "I'll pick you up next *Sunndaag* at two o'clock and I'll have something special planned."

In a saccharine voice that rivaled the tone Honor had

used when he'd held her bag for her, Eliza cooed, "Anything we do together will be special, Jonas."

He should have felt reassured by her sentiment, but he didn't trust the abrupt shift in her demeanor. Also, she was speaking too loudly for someone who'd claimed she wanted to keep their courtship private. It seemed as if she wanted Freeman and Honor to hear her. Jonas could only think of one reason for that: she was trying to make his brother envious that they were walking out.

Neh, that's narrish, he told himself. She already had the opportunity to walk out with him—or at least, to accept a ride home from him—and she'd turned him down. Then again, maybe now that she'd spent more time with Freeman, had she changed her mind? Or was the volume of her voice simply a reflection of her enthusiasm about going out alone with him? It was irritating to Jonas that he felt he had to keep second-guessing her motives, yet something about her behavior just didn't add up. But he forced himself to respond. "*Gut.* I'll see you then."

Turning to saunter away, Eliza gave him an over-the-shoulder smile. "Hopefully we'll see each other on the *bauerei* this week, too."

"I'll keep an eye out for you," Jonas replied. As he returned her smile, he thought, *Two can play this game...* even though he couldn't be sure whether she was actually playing a game or not.

Chapter Six

"*Guder mariye,* Mary," Eliza and four of her little brothers sang out together as they saw her coming up the lane on Wednesday morning. It had been raining since Monday, so it was the first time this week they were able to go blueberry picking. After being cooped up in the house for what seemed like a long time, they were all glad to be outside again and were eager to start their trek to the farm.

"*Guder mariye.*" Mary bent down and patted Eli's head. The four-year-old was sitting in a red wagon, with an empty pail for transporting the berries home on his lap. "Are you coming to pick *blohbiere,* too?" she asked him.

"*Jah,*" he exclaimed.

Samuel elaborated, "He's not tall like me because he's only four and I'm six. So he can't reach the high *biere*. But I'm going to show him how to pick the low *biere*."

"That's very helpful of you," Mary said. "Is Eli going

to be kind in return and let you ride in the wagon with him?"

"*Neh.* I don't need a ride. I'm going to run with my other *breider.*" Samuel promptly galloped off to catch up with his older brothers, who were already starting down the dirt lane.

"My *mamm* is feeling under the weather and Mark has a slight fever, too. I thought it would be a *gut* idea if I brought Eli with us so she and Mark could rest." Eliza pulled the wagon behind her as the women began walking. Speaking in *Englisch* so Eli couldn't understand, she said, "I've been curious to hear about how it went on *Sunndaag.* Did you enjoy being in the canoe alone with Freeman? Did the two of you get a chance to chat?"

"*Neh.* Not really. He was too focused on racing you, Honor and Jonas back to the other side of the lake."

"*Ach.* That's exactly what I thought may have happened, especially when I saw how fast you two were paddling."

"I don't think we were paddling any faster than Honor and Jonas were," Mary answered modestly, as usual. "I think we were quicker because we had one less person in our canoe."

"That's what Honor said, too. She seemed a little indignant that you and Freeman beat us." Eliza muttered beneath her breath, "I guess it was hard for her to accept that she and Jonas weren't as *gut* of a paddling team as she thought they were."

"Is that envy I hear in your voice, Eliza?" Mary asked, gently reproaching her.

"Why would I be envious?"

"Because Jonas seemed to be paying more attention to Honor than to you."

Uh-oh, did Mary notice that, too? "Well, it did bother me a little that Honor was being such a flirt, but I wouldn't say I was envious. I think Jonas was just being careful about how much he talked to me so no one would guess we're courting. Because when he let me off at my *haus*, he made a point of mentioning he wanted to go out alone with me next *Sunndaag*. So it's not as if I'm worried that he'd prefer to be Honor's suitor instead, or anything like that." Even as she was speaking, it occurred to Eliza that she was trying a little too hard to assure Mary that she wasn't concerned.

"That's *gut*." Mary chuckled to herself. "Although I have to admit, I'd rather Honor pursue Jonas than Freeman. She's so determined that I'd never stand a chance if he became the object of her affection."

"Well, you *might* stand a chance if you opened up to Freeman a little," Eliza suggested, repeating her earlier advice. "Give him a little sign that you're interested."

"You mean I should act like Honor does around *menner*? No, *denki*," Mary said firmly.

"You don't have to be that bold. But maybe you could... I don't know. Bring him some *blohbier* pie? He said he loved it...and you know your pie is so much better than anything Honor could ever make."

"You're *baremlich*," Mary said, but she giggled.

"*Neh*, I'm just being honest. One taste of your pie and Freeman would literally be eating out of your hand." Eliza playfully cautioned, "Just please don't give Jonas any, or he'll fall for you, too. Then you'll have both

Kanagy *breider* vying for your attention, and who would that leave me for a suitor?"

"Oh, I wouldn't worry about that if I were you," Mary said wistfully. "If Jonas ever ended your courtship, there'd be someone in line right behind him eager to become your suitor."

Jah, that's what I'm afraid of—and it would be Willis Mullet, Eliza thought. *And that's why I'm not going to let Jonas break up with me...even if it means acting bolder and more flirtatious than Honor acts.*

Jonas stepped out of the barn, smack into Honor's path. She was carrying a flowered plastic container similar to the one she'd given him on Sunday.

"There you are, Jonas. Emily told me she saw you go into the barn. I have something for you." She held out the container and Jonas hesitated to take it. Even if Honor was the best baker in all of the New Hope district, he would have been reluctant to accept whatever goodies she was offering because he didn't want to do anything to encourage her apparent interest in him. But neither did he want to be rude, so when she pushed the container into his hand, he accepted it. "It's *blohbier kaffi kuche*. I figured the muffins I made you on *Sunndaag* are long gone by now."

"*Jah*, you're right, they are." Jonas had fed them to the chickens, who'd gobbled them up in no time. "That was thoughtful of you. I'll, um, I'll just tuck them back into the barn so they aren't sitting out in the sun. I don't have time to run over to the *haus* to put them inside."

"That's a *gut* idea. Maybe we can enjoy one together later, when you're ready for a *kaffi* break. I'll be here on the *bauerei* picking *biere* for a while, so just give me a shout." Before Jonas could tell her he wasn't planning to take a coffee break, something caught Honor's attention. "Look, there's Eliza and Mary. I'm going to try to catch up with them so I have someone to chat with while I'm picking."

She flew across the dirt driveway calling their names, and Jonas went back into the barn and set the container of blueberry coffee cake inside an empty wheelbarrow by the door. Then he hastily made his way to the western corner of the farm, carrying the jar of nails he'd forgotten the first time he'd gone into the barn to retrieve his hammer and some boards.

Earlier that morning, he'd discovered a portion of the fence around the perimeter of the property had been damaged in the previous night's thunderstorm. The wind had snapped a large, rotting branch off a maple tree and it had landed on the fence, breaking several boards. Jonas had spent the early morning hours cutting up and clearing away the fallen limb. Now it was necessary to repair the fence, which discouraged deer from visiting the blueberry farm.

It's too bad I can't build a fence to keep the birds away, too, he thought as he began replacing the splintered boards. While some people recommended netting, it was too expensive and time-consuming to install on a farm this size. He'd spoken to an *Englisch* farmer who'd told him that birds were able to tear or peck their way through it to get to the fruit, anyway. The reflective scare tape Jonas and Freeman had used apparently didn't work as well when the sun wasn't out, either—

they'd found evidence the birds had been eating the berries during the rainy weather.

So Freeman had insisted on buying several rubber snakes, as well as a plastic red-tailed hawk, to use in addition to the scare tape. The problem with using fake predators was that they frequently needed to be moved so the birds wouldn't get used to them being in the same spot and figure out they weren't real.

It occurred to Jonas that he was a bit like a scarecrow himself, trying to keep Eliza from getting too close to Freeman or vice versa. *I've got to keep on my toes so they don't realize* I'm *a phony, too,* he thought. *And that includes coming up with a special date for this* Sunndaag.

He'd been brainstorming about it ever since he'd dropped off Eliza at her house, but so far, the only activity he knew she'd really like was canoeing on the lake. But that didn't seem very original, since they'd just been there with their peers. He supposed they could go for a hike at the gorge, although that wasn't exactly a unique outing, either. In fact, hiking there was such a popular Sabbath recreational activity that they were bound to meet their peers or other district members out on the trails. So Jonas mentally crossed that option off his list, too.

Why did I ever say I'd plan something special? he asked himself. *Now she's going to have high expectations, even if she did claim she'd consider anything we did together to be special.* But Jonas didn't know her well enough to come up with an activity or a destination that he was certain she'd really enjoy. It was getting to the point where he wondered if pretending to court her was worth the stress it was causing him. *Maybe I should just step aside and let my* breider *find out the hard way what Eliza is really like*, he mused.

But just last evening Freeman had mentioned Sarah, his fiancée who had died. It was during the thunderstorm and he'd remarked that she'd always relished it when storms rolled across the plains in Kansas. Freeman had commented that she'd said she'd liked it because the thunder and lightning were such remarkable displays of God's power and majesty. "I still think of her whenever it storms…" he'd admitted, his voice trailing off as he stared absently out the window.

Recalling how doleful he had sounded, Jonas knew he couldn't back out of his courtship with Eliza. Freeman was still too emotionally vulnerable. As his older brother, Jonas would always consider it his responsibility to try to protect him from getting hurt, no matter how old they were.

By the time he'd finished repairing the fence, Jonas still didn't have any clue where he'd take Eliza on Sunday. *Maybe I should go find her now and just ask her what she'd prefer to do*, he thought, since that seemed like the most practical solution. But then he'd run in to Honor, too, and she'd probably invite Mary, Eliza and her brothers to join them for coffee cake in the barn. Worse, she'd suggest that she and Jonas should go take a break alone and Eliza would hear. *I'm still trying to make up for canoeing alone with Honor on* Sunndaag. *I don't want to upset the apple cart again*, he lamented to himself.

So on his way back to the barn with the extra boards, he circumvented the section of the barrens where the customers were picking today. Instead, he cut through an area that was still off-limits and continued brooding. *How did I get myself into a position in which I'm avoiding not one but two* weibsleit *on my own* bauerei?

"You *buwe* have done a *gut* job. Those *biere* are nice and plump and I don't see any green ones," Eliza said as she surveyed the fruit the boys had picked. After helping Eli and Samuel untie their baskets, she told her four brothers, "I packed a snickerdoodle for each of you, so you can have a rest in the shade beneath those trees at the end of the row. Mary and I will be done in a few minutes and then we'll go home."

After the boys had trotted away to enjoy their snack, Honor said, "It's probably almost time for me to *absatz*, too. I brought Jonas some *blohbiere kaffi kuche*, and we're supposed to take a break together."

"You and Jonas?" Eliza echoed incredulously.

"*Jah.* Why is it so surprising he enjoys my company? Is it just because I'm a few years older than he is?"

Eliza glanced to her right at Mary, who discreetly rolled her eyes. Deep down, Eliza suspected that it was probably Honor, not Jonas, who had initiated getting together with him for a piece of coffee cake. But it still rankled Eliza and she knew she had to say something to put an end to Honor's pursuit of him. Exaggerating her pout, she said, "Your age has nothing to do with it. I'm surprised Jonas would agree to take a break alone with you because he's walking out with *me*."

"He *isn't*!" Honor exclaimed, clapping her hand over her mouth. Mary didn't even bother to pretend that this was the first she'd ever heard that Eliza and Jonas were courting.

"*Jah*, he is. He asked to be my suitor a couple of weeks ago."

"Oh, Eliza. I'm so sorry," Honor apologized. "I never would have asked him to take a *kaffi* break with me if I had known you two were courting. I feel *baremich*."

I knew she was the one who initiated it, Eliza thought. But Honor's apology sounded so heartfelt that she couldn't hold the trespass against her. "We were doing our best to keep it a secret, so you're not the one who should feel *baremlich*—Jonas should. I can't understand why he'd agree to spend time alone with you, knowing that it might give you the impression he's not already courting someone. Namely, *me*," she stressed.

She wasn't truly annoyed at him, nor was she even perplexed. Eliza had witnessed Honor's behavior around bachelors often enough to understand if Jonas had felt cornered. But she had to at least act put out, the way she might have felt if she'd authentically liked him as a suitor.

"Please don't be angry at Jonas on my account," Honor pleaded. "To be fair, I didn't really give him much of a choice in the matter." Her eyes began to well, so Eliza reached over and patted her shoulder.

"I believe you. I suppose I don't even need to mention it to him. It's a simple misunderstanding, that's all. It's nothing to get so upset about."

"That's not what I'm upset about. I'm upset because no matter how hard I try or how clever my schemes are or how often I create opportunities for the singles in our district to socialize, I still don't have a suitor. I feel like I'm never going to have one." Honor sniffled and blotted her eyes with the hem of her apron.

"I know how you feel, Honor," Mary admitted, leaning forward to see past Eliza. "It's difficult to want something so much and not know if you'll ever have it."

"*Jah*, I've been asking *Gott* to bless me with a suitor for years and years. It makes me question whether He wants me to get married and have *kinner*. I start to wonder if I should stop asking and accept that the answer is *neh*."

As Eliza listened to her friends share their disappointment, she was struck by the realization that they both dearly wanted a suitor and she dearly wished she *didn't* have one. It didn't seem fair. She was already doing everything she could to help Mary foster a connection with Freeman, but what could she do to help Honor? *Should I break up with Jonas so he can court her?* she wondered.

Yet Eliza couldn't bring herself to entertain that idea for very long. She hated to admit it, but her fear of winding up with Willis was too great. Besides, there was no guarantee that Jonas would want to court Honor if he wasn't courting Eliza.

"I don't think you should stop asking the Lord for what you want," she advised. "And I'll pray about it for you, too."

"*Denki*." Honor wiped her hands on her apron. "All right, I'm done picking for the day. Now that I know Jonas is courting you, I'm so embarrassed that I just want to leave the *bauerei* before he sees me again."

Her friends said goodbye to her, and a few minutes later Eliza announced it was quitting time. "These *bloh-*

biere are practically falling into my basket, so I wish I didn't have to leave. But I'd better bring the *buwe* home for lunch."

"I only need about a cup and a half more," Mary said, plucking handfuls of ripe fruit from the branches as she stepped farther down the aisle. "By the time you round up your *breider*, I'll be ready to go, too."

"Okay." Eliza exited the row of blueberry bushes and she was adding her basket to the other baskets in the wagon when Mary let out an ear-piercing shriek.

Jonas distinctly heard a woman scream and he charged in the direction of the noise. Halfway across the barrens, he discovered Eliza peering down a row, her hand covering her mouth. Three of Eliza's brothers were clustered behind her, the smallest one holding on to the skirt of her dress as he peeked down the row.

"What's the matter?" Jonas asked, looking over her shoulder to see what she was seeing. Peter, Eliza's oldest brother, was inching down the path between the blueberry bushes wielding a long stick.

"Mary saw a snake," Eliza answered softly without turning around. "She said it's right in front of her and she's too afraid to back away."

Indeed, some twenty feet beyond Peter, Mary was standing as still as a statue. She had one foot in front of the other; apparently she'd been in the middle of taking a stride when she'd become paralyzed by fear.

"Peter, don't go any farther," Jonas instructed the young boy. There weren't poisonous snakes in Maine, but he still didn't want the child to accidentally provoke the creature into biting him. "Just stay right there. I'm coming down the aisle behind you. Don't make any sudden movements."

Jonas crept toward Peter and took the stick from his hand. He figured he'd use it to push the snake out of Mary's path. The thick, coiled reptile was partially obscured by the long grass, but from what Jonas could tell, it had a dark zigzag pattern on its back. It actually looked a lot like a rattlesnake he'd seen once in Kansas, but Jonas knew that was impossible; there weren't any rattlesnakes in Maine. Even so, he proceeded cautiously, tiptoeing past Peter and down the aisle, holding the long stick out to one side. He was halfway to Mary when he heard his brother's voice from behind him, at the end of the row.

"I heard a scream. Is someone hurt?"

"Neh," Eliza replied. "There's a snake blocking Mary's way. She's too scared to move and the snake won't budge, either."

"It *can't* budge—it's not real!" Freeman hooted with laughter.

By this time, Jonas was within a few feet of the serpent and he could clearly see that it was one of the toy snakes his brother had mentioned he'd purchased at the discount store in town. But Mary was still frozen in the same position, so Jonas comforted her. "It's not real, Mary. It's rubber. See?"

When he tapped on the snake with the stick to demonstrate, the toy bounced a little, causing Mary to flinch. She was so pale that for a second Jonas thought she might faint. Instead, she burst into tears, twirled around and bolted down the aisle in the opposite direction so quickly that she jostled the basket still tied to her waist, scattering berries in her wake.

Jonas felt awful that his brother's careless placement of the snake had resulted in Mary being so frightened. And he felt even worse that Freeman had laughed about it. He turned around to address him, but Eliza beat him to it. Actually, she was addressing her little brothers, but her remark was clearly intended for Freeman.

"*Kumme, buwe.* It's not kind to laugh at another person when they're scared or upset, and I don't want you to ever do that. Do you understand me?" All the boys nodded except for the littlest one, Eli, who was reaching up to let Eliza put him in the wagon along with their baskets of berries. "Let's go make sure Mary's okay."

"I'm sorry, Eliza. I didn't mean—" Freeman began, but she cut him off.

"I'm not the one you should be apologizing to," she snapped as she started down the center aisle with him close on her heels. "But I doubt Mary wants to speak to you right now, so please stop following us."

"*Jah.* Okay. I'll speak to her later." Freeman took off his hat and wiped his brow as he watched Eliza and her brothers tramp toward the checkout booth. When he turned to face his brother, his cheeks were red and his eyes were clouded. "I wouldn't have placed this snake here if I knew anyone was going to be picking in this section today. I thought we agreed to direct customers to the eastern half of the barrens until tomorrow or the next day."

"I know you didn't do it on purpose." Jonas sighed. "But you really shouldn't have laughed at Mary when she was already upset."

"I wasn't laughing at Mary!" Freeman protested. "I was laughing at *you*. It was funny to see such a big strong man tiptoeing down the aisle and brandishing a stick to fend off a *toy* snake!"

"I wasn't *brandishing* the stick, I was just carrying it so I could direct the snake away from Mary. Besides, I didn't know it wasn't real at the time," Jonas reminded him, but he had to chuckle, too. "I suppose I can see why you thought I looked pretty funny, though."

"And I can see why the *weibsleit* thought I was laughing at Mary," Freeman acknowledged ruefully. "Do you think I should try to catch them before they leave so I can apologize?"

"*Neh*. Like Eliza said, Mary probably needs a little time to recover. She's likely embarrassed, and if you talk about it right now, she may feel even worse," Jonas suggested. His brother hung his head, looking so dejected that Jonas felt bad for him. But he felt even worse knowing that deep down, he was kind of relieved Freeman had fallen out of favor with Eliza.

Almost immediately, Jonas regretted having such thoughts about his brother, so he offered, "Listen, you can take these boards and nails back to the barn and I'll go smooth things over with the *weibsleit* for you."

"Are you okay, Mary?" Samuel asked, tugging her hand when the group caught up with her near the checkout booth.

"*Jah*." She glanced down and gave him a weak smile. "I feel a little *lappich*, though. Whoever heard of being afraid of a toy snake?"

"I thought it was real, too," Peter said, consoling her.

"And I was a little bit scared also, because it didn't look like any snake I ever saw before."

Mary affectionately patted his shoulder. "You were very brave, Peter. *Denki* for being willing to protect me."

"You're *wilkom*," Peter said. "I can carry your basket of berries to the scale for you, too."

"I'll pull the wagon," Isaiah offered. So Eliza allowed the boys to hurry off in front of them toward the checkout booth.

"They're such sweet, thoughtful *buwe*," Mary remarked. "Unlike some *menner* who are three times their age."

"*Jah*, I was surprised by how Freeman acted, too," Eliza agreed. "It was immature, as well as rude."

"I thought he was different than that, but maybe it's better I found out what he's really like now, before I got my hopes up that he might make a *gut* suitor." There was a hint of disappointment in Mary's voice that showed she'd *already* gotten her hopes up. So even though Eliza was offended by Freeman's behavior toward her friend, she suggested Mary not give up on him altogether.

"I know he shouldn't have laughed, but sometimes *menner* just have a different sense of humor than *weibsleit* do. I think he felt really bad that he hurt your feelings. He started to say he was sorry but I wouldn't let him finish."

"Nice of him to apologize to you, but you weren't the one who was utterly humiliated after being scared half to death," Mary pointed out.

"He wanted to apologize to you, but I told him you

probably didn't want to talk to him right now. I figured you needed to gather your composure first." Eliza couldn't help but giggle as she added, "Meanwhile, it will do him *gut* to sweat it out a little, not knowing whether you'll accept his apology or not."

"Of *course*, I'll accept his apology, because the Bible tells us to forgive one another just as *Gott* in Christ has forgiven us," Mary asserted. "But that doesn't necessarily mean I'd want him for a suitor anymore."

"Don't make up your mind just yet," Eliza advised. "Because now that Honor knows Jonas and I are courting, she might turn her focus on Freeman and then you'll regret not giving him another chance."

"I doubt that Honor would ever like Freeman. He wasn't very polite to her about her *blohbier* muffins, either."

Eliza couldn't argue with that, so she continued walking in silence until they reached the long line at the checkout booth. By the time they'd paid for their fruit, little Eli was asleep in the back of the wagon. The other three *buwe* were energized from their snickerdoodles and they abandoned the responsibility of pulling him in favor of springing alongside the driveway like grasshoppers.

Just as they reached the end, Eliza heard Jonas's voice, as he called, "Eliza, Mary, wait!"

They stopped and turned to see him jogging in their direction. In one hand, he held a large plastic jug. In the other, he was carrying a flowered container that Eliza immediately recognized as belonging to Honor's mother. *That must be the* blohbier kaffi kuche *she made for him. I hope he's not going to be as rude as his* bruder *was and ask us to give the* kuche *back to her.*

"I wanted to be sure you're all right, Mary," he said, squinting against the sun at her. "You had a bad fright and I thought you might need something to eat or drink."

Mary smiled at him. "I'm fine, *denki*. And I appreciate the offer but I'm going to have lunch soon, anyway."

"Are you sure?" he said and when Mary nodded, Jonas asked, "What about you, Eliza? Or the *buwe*?"

"*Neh*. We'd better not. As Mary said, it's almost time for lunch and a treat would spoil their appetites."

"Oh, okay." Jonas seemed disappointed and Eliza didn't know if it was because they'd turned down his hospitality or because he'd hoped to get rid of the muffins. But she thought his gesture was kind, either way. "Well, I—I also wanted to say how sorry I am about what happened. We never would have put that deterrent where we knew someone was going to be picking. We didn't intend for anyone to harvest that section until tomorrow."

"There was a group of *Englisch* teenagers picking in the eastern area," Eliza explained. "They were pretty boisterous and I was concerned about the kind of language they were using. I didn't want the boys to hear it, so Emily said we could move to the other section. Not that it's her fault—I was the one who cajoled her into it."

"I'm *hallich* you moved—I wouldn't have wanted you or your *breider* to hear foul language," Jonas said, knitting his eyebrows in consternation. "If that happens again, please let me know. I'll remind the customers that this is a *familye bauerei*. I'm sorry you had to listen to that kind of talk, even for a moment. And I'm sorry about the rubber snake, too. My *bruder* also wants to apologize for his response, but I'll let him do that in person the next time you're here… You will be coming back, won't you?"

Moved by how concerned and apologetic Jonas was, Eliza answered, "*Jah*. Of course, we'll *kumme* back, won't we, Mary?"

"I suppose that depends on how many more pies I need to make," Mary answered noncommittally. Then she pointed to Peter, who was attempting to climb a tree at the end of the lane by standing on the fence railing. "Looks like the grasshoppers have decided they'd rather be squirrels instead."

"*Ach*. Would you mind keeping an eye on them, Mary? I need to rearrange these *biere* so they don't tip over if Eli shifts positions in his sleep." She gestured to the pails they'd brought to transport the berries home.

"Sure. 'Bye, Jonas."

"'Bye, Mary." He lifted the jug in a sort of wave, and as Mary walked toward the boys, he asked Eliza, "You need a hand with those?"

"Please. I just need to make sure they're nice and snug."

Jonas set down the muffins and plastic jug. They both reached for one of the pails at the same time and his palm momentarily covered Eliza's. On Sunday, he'd taken her hand when she'd asked him to help her out of the canoe, and again when he'd assisted her out of the buggy. So why did his touch suddenly make her feel so tremulous? And why didn't the feeling pass even after he'd lifted his hand from atop hers and reached for a different container?

"There," he said, after expertly repositioning the pails. "They should be nice and secure now."

"Denki." Eliza looked into his eyes, which were more green than gray in this light. "And *denki* for coming to check on Mary. That was thoughtful of you."

"No need to thank me. I do hope the, ah, incident with the snake won't keep her from returning to the *bauerei.*"

"I think she just has to get over feeling *lappich* about being afraid of a fake snake."

"She has nothing to feel *lappich* about—I'm the one who was preparing to fend it off with a stick." Jonas chuckled at himself. "It looked like a rattlesnake I saw out on the prairie in Kansas once."

"Really?" Eliza gulped. "Did you fend that off with a stick, too?"

"Neh. I backed slowly but surely away. And as soon as I'd put enough distance between us, I hightailed it out of there like a black-tailed jackrabbit."

"Schmaert mann!" Eliza said with a chuckle. She appreciated Jonas's candid admission of how fearful he'd been, and she wished she could ask him more about the wildlife in Kansas. But she could see that Mary was having a difficult time wrangling her brothers. Gesturing toward the group, she remarked that she probably should get going now.

"Jah, me, too." Jonas bent down and picked up the plastic jug and container of muffins. When he straightened up again, he said, "But I look forward to continuing our conversation the next time we see each other."

"You want to talk more about snakes?" Eliza teased.

She couldn't help herself; she just felt very lighthearted all of a sudden. But she made Jonas blush.

"*Neh*, I meant—" he began.

"It's okay. I know what you meant—and I feel the same way. I'm really looking forward to talking more to you, too, Jonas." And for the first time since he'd asked to be her suitor, there was nothing phony or exaggerated about her sentiment.

Chapter Seven

"Mamm?" Eliza placed her hand on her mother's shoulder. Lior was snoring softly, her head tucked into her folded arms on the table. *"Mamm?"*

She roused and rubbed her eyes. "Did I fall asleep?"

"Jah. Why don't you go lie down while I get supper ready?" Eliza suggested. Over the week, her mother had become increasingly fatigued as the flu drained her energy. Now, on Saturday, she could barely keep her head up.

"I can't. I've got to finish reconciling these accounts."

Eliza doubted she had the presence of mind to calculate the charges for Uri's customers accurately. *How could he possibly expect* Mamm *to do the bookkeeping in her condition?* she wondered. *He should just wait until* Muundaag. *Better yet, he should do it himself.*

"I can take care of the books after the *buwe* go to bed," Eliza offered.

"Denki, but *neh.* You've got your hands full looking after your *breider."*

Peter, Isaiah and even little Samuel had spent the better part of the day helping Uri clean the workshop. Eli was now sick with the flu, too, just like Mark. So all five of the boys would undoubtedly be exhausted and go to bed early, leaving Eliza plenty of time to work on the accounts. So she knew her mother was just making an excuse; the real issue was that Uri didn't want anyone except Lior to manage his books.

Eliza understood it was useless to try to persuade her to relinquish the responsibility. But with some persistent coaxing, she at least managed to convince her to lie down until supper was ready after all. "You'll be able to think more clearly once you've had a *gut* rest and a bowl of *hinkel supp*."

The weather was so hot and humid that the mere mention of soup made Eliza wish she could go dip her feet in Little Loon Lake again. Thinking about the lake made her think about Jonas, which in turn made her curious about what he had planned for their "special" date.

After setting a glass of water on her mother's nightstand and checking on Eli and Mark, Eliza returned to the kitchen and began preparing soup for her mother and youngest brothers. She was also making meat loaf and mashed potatoes for Uri and the three older boys. She intended to make plenty so she could reheat the leftovers tomorrow, since cooking full meals was prohibited on the Sabbath.

As she peeled the potatoes, Eliza's thoughts strayed again to her date with Jonas the following day. Ordinarily, she might have used her mother's illness as a convenient excuse to stay home and avoid spending time alone with a suitor, especially so early in a courtship.

But in this instance, even though she had a legitimate reason to cancel her date with Jonas, she decided not to.

Uri isn't working tomorrow, so he can take care of Mamm *and the* buwe. *Maybe if he has to manage the household on his own, he'll have a better sense of how challenging it can be*, she thought. *Then he won't insist I get married and move away or find a full-time job outside the* haus.

But Eliza knew that was the wrong attitude to have toward her stepfather. Furthermore, the real reason she didn't want to miss her date had very little to do with Uri—it was that she honestly *did* hope to get to know Jonas better. In her eager anticipation, she wondered whether she should take her own advice to Mary and make a *blohbier* dessert for them to enjoy during their outing. And since he was going to the trouble of planning a special activity for them, she resolved to make the dessert a special one, too.

Eliza was leafing through her recipe cards when the mudroom door opened and Uri stumbled into the kitchen, leaning on Peter and Isaiah's shoulders. His expression was grim and his breath labored. Eliza's stomach dropped and she was instantly wracked with guilt for all of the ungenerous thoughts she'd been entertaining about him.

"What is it? Are you injured?" she asked as she helped ease him into a kitchen chain.

"I think I have the flu," he answered grimly. "It just hit me like a ton of bricks."

"Oh, *neh*!" Eliza uttered, both in sympathy for Uri and in disappointment for herself. Now there was no way she could go out with Jonas tomorrow.

* * *

On Sunday afternoon, Jonas set the bag containing marshmallows, graham crackers and chocolate bars beside him on the buggy seat. He'd already put his tackle box and two fishing rods in the back of the carriage. After agonizing over what "special" activity he and Eliza could enjoy together, he'd finally decided to take her fishing in Crooked Creek. Afterward, they'd roast marshmallows over a campfire.

Fishing isn't exactly a popular courting activity, he conceded a few minutes later as he guided his horse along the main thoroughfare. *Most people usually don't roast marshmallows or have campfires until after dark, and I intend to take Eliza back to her home long before then.* But unless another, better idea struck him between now and the time he arrived at her house, he had no choice but to carry out his plan and hope she'd enjoy herself.

Otherwise, she might not give me the chance to go out with her again, Jonas thought. But his desire to show Eliza a pleasant afternoon wasn't simply because he was worried she might break up with him. He also wanted her to have a good time because *he* wanted to have a nice afternoon *with* her. Just because their courtship wasn't real didn't mean they couldn't have *schpass* as friends. And it didn't mean he had to dread spending time with her, either.

Jonas hadn't seen Eliza—or Mary, for that matter—back on the farm since the incident with the rubber snake. But since then, he'd reflected on the conversation they'd had that morning many times. He couldn't put a finger on it, but something about Eliza seemed different as they'd talked that day. She seemed more natural somehow, as if she wasn't making such an effort or being flirtatious. And he didn't feel as if he had to work so hard to come up with small talk, either.

It reminded him of the few times they'd socialized together shortly after he had arrived in New Hope, before he'd had any notion of pretending to court her. On those occasions, he'd share what he missed about Kansas and she'd tell him what she enjoyed most about living in Maine.

That's the kind of light, relaxed conversation I hope we have today, Jonas mused, turning down the side road leading to her house. As agreed, he waited at the end of the lane for her, a common practice for young Amish men and women who didn't want their families to know they were courting. With the exception of telling his brother he was Eliza's suitor, Jonas intended to do his best to protect their privacy. So he was caught off guard when Peter and Isaiah came loping down the lane at quarter past two, fifteen minutes later than Eliza had agreed to meet him. Samuel was trailing them in the distance.

"*Guder mariye,* Jonas," Peter and Isaiah greeted him.

"Hello, *buwe,*" he replied, wondering the best way to explain why he was idling in his buggy at the end of their lane. However, he quickly learned there was no need for an explanation.

"Eliza wanted me to give you this." Peter reached up and handed him an envelope. Puzzled, Jonas tore it open. The note inside read:

Jonas,
My mother, Uri, Eli and Mark are all ill with the
flu, so I'm afraid I have to stay home and take
care of them. I'm sorry. I know you had something
special planned and I was really looking forward
to spending the afternoon together.
I hope to see you again soon.
Eliza
PS Don't worry, the boys are too young to suspect we're courting.

Jonas pushed back his hat to scratch his head. He
couldn't help it—the first question that entered his mind
was, *Is her* familye *really so sick that she has to stay
home to care for them? Or did she have a change of
heart about going out alone with me and her* familye's
illness was just a convenient excuse? He regretted not
trusting Eliza enough to take her at her word, but he
still had his doubts.

"Let's go back to the *haus*," Peter told Isaiah.

"But Eliza said we should wait to see if Jonas wants
to give her a message, too."

"Bobbelmoul!" Peter elbowed Isaiah. "She said we
weren't supposed to *ask* for a message—we were only
supposed to wait to see if Jonas *offered* her one. Otherwise, it's rude, like asking for a piece of *kuche* when
you go to someone's *haus*."

Jonas smiled to himself. He could tell from Eliza's
words to her brothers that she was hoping for a response
from him. And that meant she truly must have been
disappointed she'd had to cancel their plans. "I actu-

ally would like you to give her a message, but I need a second to think what I want you to tell her."

Isaiah raised his hat and slid a pencil from behind his ear. "Eliza said if you wanted to give her a message, you should write it instead of tell us because we might get distracted chasing a toad or a butterfly and we'd forget by the time we got back."

Now Jonas was really grinning. *Eliza is so hopeful I'll reply to her message that she even made sure her* breider *took a pencil with them so I could write back to her.* He hopped out of the buggy and accepted the pencil from Isaiah. Jonas was about to start writing when he noticed Samuel shuffling toward them, his head hanging so low that his chin nearly touched his chest.

He called hello and when the little boy glanced up, Jonas could see that his eyes were watery and his eyelids were swollen. He couldn't tell if he was coming down with the flu, too, or if he'd been crying. "Are you okay? You look a little under the weather."

Samuel tipped back his head and squinted at the sky, obviously confused by the idiom. "What weather? It's sunny out."

Jonas suppressed a chuckle, but Peter and Isaiah laughed aloud...although not unkindly.

"Jonas doesn't mean the real weather," Isaiah explained knowingly. "It's just a saying. It means you look like you're about to cry."

Samuel's eyes flooded even as he protested, "I do *not.*" He dropped his head again and kicked a pebble to the side of the driveway.

"He's upset because he didn't get to carry Eliza's note," Peter said quietly.

"Or the pencil," Isaiah added.

"I am *not*." Samuel lifted his head, his chin quivering. "I'm sad because *Daed* is sick and he can't take us to the lake and now I'll never get to go canoeing."

"Remember what Eliza told you?" Peter asked. "She said you can go when *Daed* gets better."

"What if he doesn't ever get better?" Samuel wailed.

Recognizing that the child was at least as upset about his father's illness as he was about his canceled canoeing excursion, Jonas was struck with an idea. *I could take the* buwe *fishing this afternoon. I'm sure it would be helpful to Eliza.* But first, he needed to get her approval. Jonas didn't want to present the idea only to have to disappoint Samuel again. "I think your *daed*—and your *mamm* and *breider*—will recover from the flu in a little while. And we should pray about that every day until they do," he suggested, touching Samuel's shoulder.

The child nodded. "That's what Eliza said, too. At breakfast we asked *Gott* to make them all better. And at lunch. But *Daed* is still sick and he can't get out of bed."

Noticing that Samuel was more worried about his father than he was about the other members of his family, Jonas assumed it must have been rare for Uri to be ill. He remembered how frightened he'd been the first time he'd ever seen his own *daed* laid up in bed; until then, Jonas had naively believed his tall, strapping father was impervious to almost any illness or injury. "It's *gut* that he's getting lots of rest because that's what will help him feel healthy and strong. But it might take a few days before he's one-hundred-percent better."

"Eliza said it might take this many." Sniffling, he

held up six fingers. "That's how many years old I am, too."

"You're *six*?" Jonas pretended to be surprised. "I didn't know you were six. I thought you were only five. But if you're six, maybe you can help me with an important task."

That seemed to perk Samuel up. He wiped his cheek and asked, "What task?"

"I need to ask Eliza something. I was going to write her a note, but I really need to talk to her in person. While I'm hitching my *gaul* could you run and ask her if she has a moment to *kumme* out to the porch so I can speak to her?"

Samuel nodded, but he looked crestfallen, as if he was disappointed because the task wasn't as important as he'd hoped it would be. So Jonas leaned down and whispered, "And here's the hard part—you have to be really careful not to let anyone else hear you, because we don't want to disturb their rest." It was true that he didn't want the child to wake anyone up, but Jonas also didn't want them to know about his request to talk to Eliza in private. If she agreed to allow him to take her brothers fishing, then he'd leave it up to her to explain why he'd dropped by the house in the first place. "Do you think you can do that?"

"*Jah*. I'll be as quiet as a mouse. Just like when we're in *kurrich* and I need to ask my *schweschder* a question," Samuel solemnly promised before he pivoted and shot up the driveway.

"Could you two show me where I can tie my *gaul*?" Jonas asked Peter and Isaiah, who readily led him to the hitching post. Then they accompanied him to the

Get ready to relax and indulge with your FREE BOOKS and more!

Claim up to FOUR NEW BOOKS & TWO MYSTERY GIFTS – absolutely FREE!

Dear Reader,

We both know life can be difficult at times. That's why it's important to treat yourself so you can relax and recharge once in a while.

And I'd like to help you do this by sending you this amazing offer of up to FOUR brand new full length FREE BOOKS that WE pay for.

This is everything I have ready to send to you right now:

Try **Love Inspired® Romance Larger-Print** books and fall in love with inspirational romances that take you on an uplifting journey of faith, forgiveness and hope.

Try **Love Inspired® Suspense Larger-Print** books where courage and optimism unite in stories of faith and love in the face of danger.

Or **TRY BOTH!**

All we ask in return is that you answer 4 simple questions on the attached Treat Yourself survey. You'll get **Two Free Books** and **Two Mystery Gifts** from each series you try, *altogether worth over $20*! Who could pass up a deal like that?

Sincerely,

Pam Powers

Harlequin Reader Service

Treat Yourself to Free Books and Free Gifts.

Answer 4 fun questions and get rewarded.

We love to connect with our readers! Please tell us a little about you...

	YES	NO
1. I LOVE reading a good book.	◯	
2. I indulge and "treat" myself often.	◯	◯
3. I love getting FREE things.	◯	
4. Reading is one of my favorite activities.	◯	◯

TREAT YOURSELF • Pick your 2 Free Books...

Yes! Please send me my Free Books from each series I select and Free Mystery Gifts. I understand that I am under no obligation to buy anything, as explained on the back of this card.

Which do you prefer?
- ❏ **Love Inspired® Romance Larger-Print** 122/322 IDL GRDP
- ❏ **Love Inspired® Suspense Larger-Print** 107/307 IDL GRDP
- ❏ **Try Both** 122/322 & 107/307 IDL GRED

FIRST NAME   LAST NAME

ADDRESS

APT.#   CITY

STATE/PROV.   ZIP/POSTAL CODE

EMAIL ❏ Please check this box if you would like to receive newsletters and promotional emails from Harlequin Enterprises ULC and its affiliates. You can unsubscribe anytime.

LI/SLI-520-TY22

▲ If offer card is missing write to: Harlequin Reader Service, P.O. Box 1341, Buffalo, NY 14240-8531 or visit www.ReaderService.com ▲

BUSINESS REPLY MAIL
FIRST-CLASS MAIL   PERMIT NO. 717   BUFFALO, NY

POSTAGE WILL BE PAID BY ADDRESSEE

HARLEQUIN READER SERVICE
PO BOX 1341
BUFFALO NY 14240-8571

NO POSTAGE
NECESSARY
IF MAILED
IN THE
UNITED STATES

porch steps before meandering around to the backyard, leaving Jonas alone to nervously await Eliza's arrival.

Eliza hummed as she pushed the rocker back and forth, cradling her youngest brother. Three-year-old Mark was the last of her "patients" to finally fall asleep. But she was concerned that if she set him down, he'd wake up again and start crying, which just might make *her* start crying, too. She'd been up half the night caring for her family and she was exhausted.

Even in her feeble condition, her mother had tried to help Eliza comfort Eli and Mark when they'd woken up crying and feverish in the middle of the night. But Lior's legs were so weak that she'd barely made it halfway up the stairs before collapsing into a sitting position. She'd made such a racket that Eliza had feared she'd actually fallen *down* the staircase. Surprisingly, Uri had never even roused; he'd been so wiped out that he'd been sleeping ever since he'd returned from the workshop on Saturday afternoon.

Thankfully, Eliza had already had the flu earlier that summer and so had the other three boys. *I don't know what I would have done without them this morning*, she thought. Peter had helped her make breakfast, Isaiah had read to Eli and Samuel had kept Mark entertained with a hand puppet so he wouldn't fuss and wake up Lior and Uri. The three boys couldn't have been more helpful. Yet after their brief home-worship service, Eliza had snapped at Peter for dropping their copy of the hymnal, *The Ausbund*, as it had narrowly missed her bare foot. And then she'd scolded Samuel for whining because Uri couldn't take him to the lake.

Of all people, I should be more understanding about how disappointed he is, because I felt the same way when I realized I couldn't go out with Jonas, she silently chastised herself. She just hoped Jonas didn't feel equally let down, especially after making special plans for their date. Eliza glanced toward the window. *I suppose the* buwe *would have* kumme *inside by now to relay a message if Jonas had asked them to pass one along.*

Just after the thought ran through her mind, she heard the door open. A few seconds later, Samuel crept into the living room. "It's okay. You don't have to tip-toe, honey," she told him. "Mark is sound asleep now."

But Samuel approached the rocking chair, then whispered, "I promised to be very quiet so no one would hear when I told you something."

"You have a secret?"

"*Neh.* A message." Even though they were the only two people in the house who were awake, Samuel cupped his hands around Eliza's ear. "Jonas wants to know if you can talk to him on the porch."

Eliza turned to face her little brother, their noses just inches apart. "He's on the porch?"

"Not yet. He's hitching his *gaul*."

Eliza had been hoping for a verbal message or a note from Jonas, but she couldn't imagine why he'd need to come talk to her on the porch, unless it was to express his annoyance that she'd canceled their plans. But he wouldn't do that, knowing her family was sick, would he? Either way, she had to find out and then send him home. What if Uri woke up and managed to drag himself out of bed and saw or heard Jonas talking to her? He'd insist Eliza tell him what was going on.

So she whispered, "*Denki* for telling me Jonas's message, Samuel. That was a big responsibility. Could you help me with something else that's a very big responsibility?"

"*Jah,*" the child agreed.

"While I go speak to Jonas, could you please stay here and listen in case *Mamm* or your *daed* or *breider* wake up? And if they do, can you *kumme* get me as quick as a bunny so I can bring them whatever they need?"

"*Jah.* I'll listen very carefully."

"*Denki.* I'll be right back."

Eliza gingerly rose, set Mark on the sofa and tucked a quilt around him. Then she hurried out to the porch, where Jonas was pacing. As soon as she'd shut the door behind her, she assured him she didn't have the flu, but suggested he might want to keep his distance as a precaution.

"It's okay. I already had that flu earlier this summer. It was awful. I hope your *familye* isn't suffering too much?"

He didn't seem annoyed that she'd canceled the date. He just looked concerned about her familye's well-being. "They're having a rough time of it, especially my *mamm.* But they'll be okay in a few days, *Gott* willing."

"I'll keep them in my prayers." Jonas shifted his stance and rubbed his jaw, which Eliza noticed was clean-shaven. Suddenly, she felt very frumpy by comparison. She'd been in such a rush to check on Eli and Mark this morning that she'd donned yesterday's apron instead of putting on a clean one. And she hadn't even looked in the mirror when she was pinning her prayer *kapp* to her hair, so for all she knew, it was crooked and she probably had blueberry jam on her face, too.

"Denki," she said. While she appreciated his concern and was glad he understood why she'd broken their date, Eliza didn't have a lot of time for chitchat. She said, "I really should go back inside to make sure my little *breider* are still asleep, so…"

"Right. I figured you might need some help or a little rest yourself. So I was wondering if I could take Samuel, Isaiah and Peter fishing at the creek for a couple of hours?"

Eliza was so taken aback she could hardly reply. She never would have imagined a suitor proposing such a generous offer, especially after she'd just canceled a date with him. "I—I couldn't ask you to do that," she stammered.

"You didn't ask. I offered. I promise I'll keep a very close eye on the *buwe*. I won't let them fall in the water or *kumme* into contact with any rattlesnakes," he said, his lips twitching with an impish smile.

"In that case, *jah*. It would really be *wunderbaar*," she said. "I know they'll love it, especially Samuel. Uri was supposed to take him canoeing for the first time today and he was crushed he couldn't go."

"So I gathered," Jonas said. "I'll round up Peter and Isaiah from the backyard, if you send Samuel out."

Eliza practically skipped into the house. Samuel was also beside himself with happiness when she told him that Jonas wanted to take him and his brothers fishing in the creek. He bounded out of the house and down the porch steps so quickly that his hat flew off. When he turned back to get it, Eliza waved at him from the doorway.

"If *Daed* wakes up, tell him I didn't go canoeing without him," he called, holding up six fingers. "I'm waiting 'til he gets better in this many days."

Hopefully it won't take that long, Eliza thought. As she watched Jonas's buggy pull down the lane, she murmured a prayer for her family's health, as well as for the boys to have an enjoyable time. Then she went into the house and lied down on the other end of the sofa where Mark was sleeping.

Just before she dozed off, she thought about how grateful she was for Jonas's presence in her life. Because while she originally may not have wanted a suitor, today she was in dire need of a nap, and she never would have been able to take one if it hadn't been for him.

When Jonas brought the boys back to their house shortly before five o'clock, Eliza was sitting on the porch swing reading to Eli and Mark. "You didn't catch anything?" she asked her empty-handed brothers as she stood up.

"*Jah*. I caught a brook trout but it was too little so I couldn't keep it," Isaiah answered.

"I caught three but they were all too little, too," Peter said.

"I caught a frog with my hands. It was almost bigger than Peter and Isaiah's fishes," Samuel boasted. "But I put it back because the creek is its home and I wouldn't want someone to pick me up out of my home and put me down someplace else."

"I see. Well, if you've been handling frogs and fishes, you'd all better go wash your hands before supper. Please help Eli and Mark wash theirs, too," Eliza instructed the boys.

Jonas had noticed how frequently they'd quoted their older sister, and he could see clearly she was like a second mother to them. *She probably wants to have* kinner *of her own soon*, he thought as the boys obeyed her request and went indoors. *She'd make a* wunderbaar *mamm.*

"Jonas?" she asked, her voice interrupting his reverie.

"I'm sorry. What did you say?"

"I said it's obvious the *buwe* had a lot of *schpass*. I hope they behaved themselves."

"*Jah*. No problems at all," he replied.

"*Gut*. I can't thank you enough for taking them to the creek. It gave me the opportunity to take a nice long nap, which I desperately needed."

"You look a lot more rested," Jonas remarked, noting that her eyes were brighter now. In fact, they appeared to be sparkling.

"*Jah*, with my stained apron and uncombed hair, I must have looked like I was coming apart at the seams earlier," she admitted, self-consciously smoothing down the skirt of her dress.

"I didn't mean that. You could be wearing a gunnysack and you'd still look pretty." The unbidden thought seemed to leap from his mind to his tongue, and once spoken, it made both of them blush.

"*Denki,*" Eliza murmured.

Jonas quickly attempted to cover up his embarrassment as he confessed, "By the way, if the *buwe* don't have big appetites, I'm to blame. I gave them s'mores for a snack."

"Wow. No wonder they're so *hallich*. Fishing in the creek and roasting marshmallows is a *wunderbaar* way for young *buwe* to spend an afternoon," she declared. "But how did you happen to have the makings for s'mores in your buggy?"

Chagrined that she considered the activities he'd planned for their date to be more suitable for young boys to enjoy, he stuttered. "I—I..."

"Oh, I see!" She giggled. "You had the treats on hand because you were planning to go fishing and roast marshmallows with *me*."

"Jah," he admitted. "I suppose that probably doesn't seem like a very special activity for adults, though."

"Are you kidding? S'mores are my favorite and going to the creek would have been so refreshing," she insisted. Peering into his eyes, she lowered her voice and added, "But being able to take a nap when I desperately needed one was more special than any other activity you could have planned, Jonas."

There was something about the sincerity of her tone and the way she was looking at him that made Jonas feel ten feet tall, and yet weak-kneed at the same time. His mouth was so dry he had to lick his lips before replying. "I'm *hallich* to hear that. But I hope I didn't put you in an awkward position with your *mamm* and Uri. I mean, because if the *buwe* mention our outing, your *eldre* will probably figure out we're courting."

"I don't mind if they know," she said with a shrug. "As long as it doesn't bother you."

"Neh. Not at all. I'm proud to be your suitor." Once

again, the words flew from Jonas's lips, but this time he didn't feel embarrassed after he said them. He felt happy—although more than a little bit vulnerable—because they were more true than not.

Chapter Eight

On Monday, Eliza ended up doing the bookkeeping for Uri, anyway. She also used his cell phone—which the *Ordnung* permitted for business purposes, provided it was used more than five hundred feet away from their house—to call customers and inform them their orders might be delayed until Uri recovered.

Thankfully, his bout of the flu passed a lot quicker than Lior's. On Tuesday morning, he startled Eliza by walking into the kitchen from the mudroom. "I didn't realize you were outside. I thought you were still sleeping," she said.

"*Neh.* I felt well enough to milk the *kuh.* Peter and Isaiah have been taking care of the livestock for the past few days, so I thought I'd let them sleep in."

"I'm *hallich* you're doing better, but I didn't expect you to recover so quickly." Eliza hesitated before telling him that she'd called a couple of his customers to explain their orders might be delayed. She had tried to speak to her parents about it first, but they were both either sleeping or too groggy throughout the day to hold a conversation. Uri was so territorial about his business that she expected him to be angry she'd made the decision to contact his customers on her own, but instead, he thanked her.

"I appreciate that you took the initiative to do that. Even though I feel okay now, I might run out of steam by lunchtime, so the orders might wind up being delayed, anyway." He averted his eyes and contemplatively stroked his beard. Eliza had rarely seen him appear self-conscious, and she thought it was because he was embarrassed that he was going to be late fulfilling orders. But then he said softly, "I—I might need your help with the bookkeeping, too. Your *mamm's* mind is too foggy to do it right now, but you've always been *gut* with numbers."

Surprised to receive both an expression of gratitude *and* a compliment from her stepfather in one morning, Eliza beamed. "I already took care of the books, too."

"You did? But I didn't give you per—" Uri began, his tone gruff. But he stopped in midsentence and simply mumbled, *"Denki."* Then he poured himself a large cup of coffee and said he would drink it on the porch until breakfast was ready.

Within minutes, everyone except Lior was seated at the table. Uri said grace, thanking the Lord for their food. When he'd finished praying, just as everyone else was lifting their heads, Samuel chimed in, "And *denki* for making *Daed* all better. Please help *Mamm* feel all better, too."

Once again, Eliza expected a stern reaction from Uri, since it was considered inappropriate for an Amish child to interject a remark into an adult's conversation, and especially into a conversation with the Lord. But something about Samuel's prayer must have touched Uri, because he reached over and tousled his hair. Then he served himself three heaping spoonfuls of breakfast casserole, a sure sign he was on the mend.

The boys quietly devoured their meals and afterward Eliza excused them from the table to go brush their teeth. "Peter, you can help Mark with his toothbrush and Isaiah can help Eli, please. Afterward, you may quietly put together a puzzle or read in the living room so you don't disturb *Mamm*'s rest."

Only Samuel remained at the table, clearly dawdling on purpose so he could talk to his father. "Guess where we went on *Sunndaag*, *Daed*." The boy didn't wait for his father to reply as he told him, "Jonas took us fishing at Crooked Creek."

Uri raised an eyebrow at Eliza. "Jonas?" he repeated.

She nodded and Samuel innocently elaborated, "He's Eliza's friend from the *blohbier bauerei*. And he's our friend, too. We had s'mores, but only one each because he didn't want Eliza or *Mamm* to be upset that they made supper and then we didn't want to eat it. 'Cept he got to have two because he doesn't have a *mamm* or wife to make him supper or *appenditlich* treats. He only has a *bruder* and his *bruder* can't bake any desserts a person would ever eat. Not even if it was the only dessert on a dessert island."

When Samuel stopped talking to take a drink of milk, Uri caught Eliza's eye and then covered his mouth with his arm, coughing into the crook of his elbow. When she rose to bring him a glass of water, she realized he wasn't coughing—he was laughing. Eliza didn't know whether it was Samuel's mangling of the phrase *deserted island* or the fact that he had clearly quoted Jonas verbatim that tickled her father's funny bone, but suddenly she could hardly suppress her own laughter. She managed to dismiss Samuel from the table before dropping into her chair and cracking up into her hand so no one else would hear.

In all the time she'd known Uri, she'd rarely seen him laugh like that, and she'd certainly never laughed that long with him. Their shared amusement made her feel closer to him, and some of her previous resentment seemed to melt away. When their laughter subsided, he pushed back his chair and stood up. "That was thoughtful of your suitor to take the *buwe* to the creek. Maybe this time you've chosen someone who'd make a *gut* match for you after all."

Normally, Eliza would have bristled at Uri's comment because she would have considered it to be intrusive. But today she took it in stride, preferring to think of it as a compliment instead of as her stepfather's attempt to pressure her into getting married. "We'll see," she replied lightly.

After Uri left for the workshop and Eliza began doing the dishes, she found she couldn't stop thinking about Jonas's positive attributes. As Uri mentioned, he was very thoughtful. He was also funny, kind and hardworking, not to mention he had an affable, easygoing way with her brothers. She could almost picture him cradling a baby of his own in his strong, muscular arms someday…

"Are you okay?" Lior touched her shoulder, startling Eliza from her daydream.

"Oh, *guder mariye, Mamm*. I'm fine," she responded. Although she was glad to see her mother out of bed and dressed in her regular clothing, Lior still had dark circles beneath her eyes. "How are *you* feeling?"

"Better. I even have a bit of an appetite this morning."

"Then sit down and I'll fix you *oier* and *kaffi*. I need a second cup myself."

"*Gut*. You can fill me in on what's been going on around here. I feel as if I've been away on a long trip. It even seems as if the *buwe* have gotten taller in my absence."

Eliza chuckled. "Considering how many *blohbiere* they've been eating lately, they probably *have* grown."

She spent the next ten minutes telling her mother about Eli and Mark's recovery from the flu, how she'd taken over the bookkeeping and customer calls for Uri and what the other three boys had been doing the last few days, including their fishing trip to the creek with Jonas. Finally, she confided, "Now I understand better why it was so meaningful to you when Uri took you shopping so you could get the ingredients for my birthday *kuche*. That kind of thoughtfulness really endears a *mann* to you, doesn't it?"

"Mmm-hmm," Lior murmured, partially obscuring her smile behind the rim of her mug.

"What are you laughing at?" Eliza asked.

"I'm not laughing. I'm smiling because I've never heard you speak so fondly about one of your suitors."

Embarrassed, Eliza poured another splash of milk into her coffee and stirred it so she wouldn't have to meet her mother's eyes. "You've hardly ever heard me talk about my suitors at all."

"Exactly. You must really like Jonas."

"I like him for as much as I know him, *jah*. But I still don't know him all that well." She was trying to remind herself of that fact as much as she was her mother. "I don't want to get carried away with my emotions just because he did one very thoughtful thing for me."

"I agree. It's *gut* to take time to get to know him better. Maybe by next *Muundaag*, I'll be feeling well enough that you can return to the *blohbier bauerei* and spend time with him again."

"Muundaag?" Eliza exclaimed. "That's almost a full week away!"

Lior burst out laughing. "I was only teasing so I could determine how eager you really are to see him."

Eliza could feel her cheeks and ears burning. She was going to insist that she'd only meant she hoped her mother would feel better long before Monday, but she couldn't deny she was also eager to see Jonas again, too. Especially since he'd left her house the other day without arranging to take her out after church this coming Sunday. It was possible he hadn't asked her out because he was going to be out of town or had other plans, but she suspected he'd simply been counting on seeing her again and asking her then. So she wanted to be sure they had another opportunity to chat before Sunday rolled around.

"You're right, *Mamm*," Eliza admitted. "I would like to see him again once you're well enough to manage the *buwe* on your own."

Lior leaned forward and took her daughter's hand. In a serious voice, she said, "I appreciate everything you do around here for me. For all of us. But there will *kumme* a day when we'll have to manage without you. It will be an adjustment, but we'll be fine. So when you're ready to get married and have a *familye*—"

"Who said anything about getting married?" Eliza protested, withdrawing her hand from her mother's. "Just because my feelings for Jonas are different from my feelings for past suitors doesn't mean I hope to marry him."

"I understand that, Eliza," her mother stated firmly. "But what I need you to understand is that when you do fall in love and want to get married and start a *familye*, you have my blessing. I wouldn't ever want to stand in the way of your happiness and *Gott's* will for your life."

Eliza slowly nodded. "I understand, *Mamm*." Rising to her feet to scramble a couple of eggs for her mother, she added, "But right now I'm perfectly *hallich* with the way things are."

Yet for the first time, when Eliza thought about what it might be like to be married, she didn't imagine it making her *un*happy.

"Is that all you're going to eat?" Freeman asked his brother on Thursday after Jonas crumpled his napkin and dropped it onto his plate. They were eating leftover barbecued chicken they'd bought from Millers' Restaurant on Wednesday evening. "You're not sick, are you?"

"Neh." Jonas wasn't physically ill, anyway. But from his previous courting experience, he recognized that he was suffering from lovesickness. Ever since Sunday, he'd lost his appetite, he'd had trouble sleeping and he couldn't stop thinking about the woman he was courting.

How did this happen? he asked himself, just as he'd done when he'd gotten the flu earlier in the summer. He'd thought he'd taken the most important precaution—namely, remaining emotionally distant—so he wouldn't fall for Eliza. In fact, he'd thought he was *immune* to her charms. But here he was, feeling almost as if he was in physical pain because he hadn't seen her for four days.

Or maybe he was achy because he recognized that his feelings for Eliza were in conflict with his better judgment. Jonas knew that his past courting experience should have been enough to deter him from becoming vulnerable to a woman again. And *Eliza's* past courting experience definitely should have reinforced his reluctance. Yet it was as if he'd lost sight of the reason he'd asked to be her suitor in the first place—because she was a heartbreaker and he didn't want his brother to get hurt. And somehow, he'd pushed the fact that this was supposed to be a fake courtship to the back of his mind.

"*Gut.* That means all the more for me." Freeman helped himself to the last two pieces of chicken. "I haven't seen Eliza on the *bauerei* this week. Did you two have an argument on *Sunndaag* or something?"

Although on Sunday Jonas had mentioned he was going to Eliza's house, he hadn't shared any other details about his afternoon with his brother. Until now, Freeman hadn't asked him about it, either. So his sudden interest in Eliza put Jonas on edge. Was his brother *hoping* Jonas wasn't getting along with her? "*Neh.* Her *familye* has the flu, so she's had to stay home to care for them. I'm sure she'll be back once her *mamm* feels better." Then he pointed out, "Not that it would be any of your business if Eliza and I *did* have an argument."

"*Neh*, it wouldn't be," Freeman agreed amiably. He speared several green beans with his fork, chewed them and swallowed, then added, "I wasn't trying to be nosy. I only wanted to know because I haven't seen Mary around here since the day she got scared by the snake. Since she's Eliza's friend, I was concerned that my behavior might have reflected poorly on you. That it might have caused a problem between you and Eliza."

Jonas relaxed his shoulders. "*Neh*. Things are going well between us. Very well."

"I'm *hallich* to hear that." Freeman didn't sound very happy, though; he sounded forlorn. Was that because he was holding out hope that things wouldn't work out for his brother and Eliza? Or was it simply because he wished he could be courting someone, too?

Jonas cleared his throat. "Did you, uh, did you meet anyone new at the singing last weekend?" On Sunday evening, Freeman had attended a big regional singing with young singles from the New Hope, Unity and Serenity Ridge districts. But until today, Jonas had deliberately avoided questioning him about it, since he hadn't wanted Freeman to turn the tables and start asking him about his date with Eliza.

"*Jah*. Lots of new people. It was three districts," Freeman answered.

"You know what I mean. Did you meet any *weibsleit* who captured your attention?"

"Look who's being nosy now!" Freeman replied, needling him. "*Neh*, I couldn't picture myself in a courtship with any of the *weibsleit* I met there."

Once again, Jonas experienced a pang of insecurity. Was Freeman uninterested in anyone else because he was still carrying a torch for Eliza? Or was it simply that he didn't seem to have anything in common with any of the young women he'd met?

As if he'd read Jonas's mind, Freeman elaborated, "I know Serenity Ridge and Unity are only a day trip from here, but I'd rather not have a long-distance courtship."

"Well, have you ever considered courting... Honor Bawell?" Jonas had just said the first single woman's name that popped into his mind, and Honor was an obvious choice since she was clearly interested in being courted.

"Honor? No way!" Freeman said, and guffawed. "I'd only want to court someone with the intention of eventually marrying her. And I could never marry Honor— I'd starve to death if she were my wife!"

Jonas had to chortle at that, then he suggested, "How about Mary Nussbaum? I don't know her very well, but since she's a friend of Eliza's, she must have some *wunderbaar* qualities."

"I have considered her, *jah*. But she barely spoke to me that day we went canoeing. And now, after what happened with the rubber snake, I doubt she'll even say hello to me again."

"Sometimes the most unlikely people make the best couples." *And I should know*, Jonas thought.

"Since when did you become New Hope's resident matchmaker?" Freeman quipped. "Just because you're smitten with Eliza doesn't mean I have to be in a courtship to be *hallich*, too."

"I never said I was smitten with Eliza!" Jonas objected.

"You didn't have to say it. It's written all over your face."

"Well, you've got barbecue sauce written all over yours," Jonas joked, getting up to take his plate to the sink. "I'm going to hit the hay."

"Already? The sun hasn't even set."

But after four nights of tossing and turning in bed, Jonas was beat. Even if he didn't wind up getting any more sleep tonight than he had gotten earlier in the week, he didn't care. All that mattered was that the next day brought the possibility he'd see Eliza on the blueberry farm. Because as soon as he saw her, he was going to ask her to go out with him after church on Sunday.

By Friday, Eliza was champing at the bit to get to the blueberry farm. She'd hoped to go on Wednesday, or Thursday at the latest. But she could see that her mother was still fatigued on Wednesday, and on Thursday, Almeda Stoll, the deacon's wife, stopped by with two meals for their family, since she'd heard Lior and the boys had been ill.

It would have been rude if Eliza hadn't offered her hospitality in return. So she'd poured sun tea and served Almeda, Lior and herself slices of the blueberry-cream-cheese cake she'd intended to bring to Jonas. Moments after Almeda left, Uri came into the house carrying two business ledgers. Apparently, Eliza and Lior had duplicated several entries and it had taken him an hour to reconcile their mistakes.

Uri had complained, "This is why only one person should work on the accounts."

It's also why you should only keep one business led-

ger, Eliza had thought. By that time, it was almost two thirty, which wouldn't have allowed her time to get to the farm, pick berries and return in time to have supper on the table by six o'clock.

On Friday morning, however, she was bound and determined to leave her house by eight, even if it meant taking all five of her brothers with her. Thankfully, it didn't come to that. Quite the opposite: Uri decided he needed Peter and Isaiah's help in the workshop. And Lior insisted the other three boys stay with her, despite Eliza's expressed concern for her mother's health. So a few minutes before eight o'clock, she started off for the farm on her own. She'd barely made it down the driveway when she spotted Mary heading toward her, swinging a big plastic bucket.

"What a *wunderbaar* surprise. It's such a treat to be able to spend time alone with you on a weekday!" Eliza exclaimed. "I was beginning to worry you'd never *kumme* picking *biere* with me again."

"To be honest, I wasn't sure I was going to return to the *bauerei*, either. But then I decided I was being prideful because I'd felt so *lappich* and that I really should give Freeman another chance." Mary giggled. "Plus, I need to make more jam to sell at the *blohbier* festival. How has the picking been this week?"

"I don't know. I haven't been back since we went last *Mittwoch*, either." Eliza explained that Uri had gotten ill, in addition to Eli, Mark and Lior. Then she told Mary about how Jonas had taken her brothers fishing at the creek on Sunday so Eliza could have a break. "Wasn't that considerate of him?"

"I suppose." Mary's response was barely audible.

"Jonas also made a campfire and they roasted marshmallows and had s'mores, since that's what he had planned for us to do on our date. The *buwe* are still talking about how much *schpass* they had."

"Apparently, they're not the only ones still talking about it."

Eliza had never heard Mary use sarcasm before and she felt stung by it. Her eyes brimming, she asked, "Why are you being like that, Mary? First you complained I acted as if it was a chore to have a suitor. And now that I'm excited about courting Jonas, you still seem critical. I thought you'd be *hallich* for me."

Turning to her, Mary immediately apologized. "*Jah*, you're right. There's no need for me to be so surly. I am *hallich* for you, Eliza. It's just that…well, it's difficult for me to hear about how *wunderbaar* Jonas is because I want a suitor to do those kinds of things for me, too." She flicked her prayer *kapp* string over her shoulder and acknowledged, "But that's a very self-centered way for me to behave. I'm sorry."

"*Ach*." Eliza groaned. "I'm the one who's being self-centered, as well as insensitive. I know how much you want a suitor and here I am, babbling on and on about Jonas. It's just that I've never felt this way about anyone I've courted before, and I feel like I can hardly contain myself. But from now on, I promise I'll try."

"*Neh*. You can't do that," Mary objected. "Otherwise if I get a suitor, I won't feel free to gush about him to you." She grinned.

"First of all, it's not *if* you get a suitor—it's *when*," Eliza emphatically corrected her. "And secondly, I'm not *gushing*."

Mary gave her a knowing look. "Okay, you might not be gushing about Jonas. But take my word for it, you're definitely *blushing.*"

Eliza didn't have to take Mary's word for it; the closer they got to the Kanagy brothers' farm, the hotter her cheeks and forehead felt. And her stomach swirled with a kaleidoscope of butterflies. In all her years of courting, she'd never been so anxious to see her suitor.

As they turned up the driveway, Eliza remarked that the parking area seemed very crowded for so early in the morning. "There are probably so many *Englisch* customers here because they're preparing their baked goods for the *blohbier* festival the weekend after this one," she ventured.

"Probably. But it also might be because next week we're supposed to get a lot of rain."

"Really? I didn't know that." Eliza was disappointed. She'd already missed seeing Jonas every day this week, and now she wouldn't see him next week, either? It made her even more eager to chat with him today and find out if he wanted to make plans with her for Sunday.

When they reached the booth to retrieve the kind of baskets they could tie around their waists, Eliza and Mary discovered a handwritten sign posted over the scale. It said:

The cashier will be unavailable to check out customers until 9:30. We apologize for the inconvenience. Please help yourselves to baskets.

There was also a map indicating which area of the farm was open for picking.

"Of all the days for Emily to be late, it's a shame

it's today, when there are so many customers here," Mary commented as they tied their baskets around their waists.

"*Jah*, that's too bad," Eliza agreed absentmindedly as she looked around for Jonas, who was nowhere in sight.

"I'm sorry—we only take checks or cash," Jonas informed the *Englisch* customer who handed him a credit card.

There was a big sign posted over the crate of baskets that plainly stated this policy. If Emily had been distributing baskets, instead of home in bed with the flu, she would have reminded the customers of this fact, too. The Kanagy brothers had always tried to make sure people understood *before* they started picking berries that credit cards would not be accepted.

Although the *Ordnung* permitted certain businesses in town to use credit-card processors, Jonas and Freeman had decided long ago they weren't going to use one. They didn't want the hassle of installing an electrical line or getting an internet connection, which so many of the machines required in order to work. Most of the local customers were accustomed to bringing checks or cash to Amish businesses and very few took issue with their payment policy. However, the woman standing in front of him was the third customer who had complained about it this morning.

"But *I* never carry cash or checks," the woman retorted. "I don't think it's fair to impose *your* religious beliefs on me. It's not a very good business practice, either."

Jonas could feel his eye twitch and he sensed a headache wasn't far away. Rather than tell the customer he wasn't trying to impose his beliefs on her, he offered, "If you'd like, I can put aside your fruit for you until you're able to return with cash or a check?"

"I don't have spare time in my schedule to be running back and forth like that!" she objected, even though she clearly had spare time in her schedule to argue with Jonas.

The woman standing beside her seemed embarrassed. "I've got plenty of cash with me, Beth. Why don't I pay for yours and you can pay me back later?"

"I'm tempted to just put this basket down and walk away in protest of the payment policy. But after all the work I put into picking these berries, I won't give him the satisfaction," she said to her friend as if Jonas couldn't hear her.

Please, Gott, *give me patience and an attitude that reflects Your mercy,* he silently prayed as he turned to set the second customer's berries on the scale.

Freeman had sometimes suggested they were overpaying Emily, who often sat idly in between checking customers in or out. He'd thought that they should give her additional responsibilities on the farm to keep her busy, such as picking berries to sell to people who wanted to buy them by the pint instead of picking their own. "We could put a bell on the booth for customers to ring when they're ready to pay for their fruit. That would alert Emily to return to her station," he'd suggested.

But Jonas had always insisted that customers would be frustrated if they had to wait for Emily to return from a distant part of the farm. Furthermore, he wanted her to remain at the booth to be a welcoming presence, to answer customers' questions and to direct them to the picking area or inform them they could get a ride in the buggy wagon. Now that Jonas had manned the booth and dealt with several unreasonable *Englischers* in Emily's absence, he had an even greater appreciation for the service she provided, both to the customers and to Jonas and Freeman. *Maybe if Freeman spends a few hours doing her job, he'll have a better understanding of how challenging it can be, too*, he thought.

But that would mean Jonas would have to switch responsibilities with him and transport customers across the farm in the buggy wagon. He was reluctant to leave the booth because he'd hoped to see Eliza the moment she arrived on the farm so he could ask her if she'd spend Sunday afternoon with him. Usually, she and her brothers didn't arrive until nine thirty or ten o'clock, but Jonas had been at the booth since nine twenty and he still hadn't seen her. Now it was almost noon and he was beginning to lose hope that she was coming to the farm at all today.

He continued weighing the fruit and collecting payments, but the line appeared to be growing longer instead of shorter. No doubt that was because most of the customers wanted to get out of the hot sun and go home to eat their lunches. While Jonas was waiting on a pleasant group of young adults wearing T-shirts from the local university, he noticed Freeman across the driveway, returning from a buggy run. He waved him to come over so they could switch places.

After the group of college students paid for their fruit and moved on, Jonas was astonished to recognize who was next in line. "Eliza and Mary, I didn't know you were here!" he exclaimed.

They both greeted him, and then Eliza explained, "We got here bright and early. We had to make up for lost time." Her skin was dewy and flushed and she had dirt smudged across her cheekbone, but she looked absolutely luminous and Jonas couldn't stop grinning. As he was weighing her fruit, she asked, "Is everything okay with Emily?"

"She has the flu."

"Ach. Poor *maedel*." Eliza clucked her tongue. "And poor you, too—it seems like a busy day to be short-staffed."

"*Jah*, but I'd rather have too many customers than too few," Jonas replied in *Deitsch*.

As they were speaking, Freeman came up beside Jonas and greeted Mary and Eliza. Then, still speaking *Deitsch*, Jonas told him it was his turn to wait on the customers and he'd give them buggy rides.

"*Gut*. I'd prefer to sit in the shade for a while. But after you drop the customers off, take a look at the left-hand corner of the barren near the woods. I think something's been eating our *biere* again," he replied, also in *Deitsch*.

"Birds?" Jonas asked.

"*Neh*. Bears."

Mary's hand flew to her cheek. "Bears?"

"Don't worry, it's probably only *one* bear. And judging from how many *biere* he ate, he'd be way too full to take a chomp out of you." Freeman chuckled nervously. Jonas knew how troubled he'd been about upsetting Mary a while back and how eager he was to apologize to her, but once again, it almost seemed as if he was making light of her fear. She pinched her lips together in a tight seam. Jonas noticed Eliza's smile had faded, too.

Thinking quickly, he said, "Most of the customers are going home for lunch, so I think I have time for a quick bottle of root beer before we have a big enough group to take a buggy ride. Would you like a cool drink before you walk home, Eliza and Mary?"

"*Jah,* please," Eliza replied.

"*Neh, denki,*" Mary answered at the same time. She quickly added, "But you go ahead, Eliza. I'll wait over there in the shade beneath that maple." She gave Freeman and Jonas a curt goodbye and started across the lawn, barely allowing Eliza time to reply.

Jonas was concerned she would change her mind and leave with Mary, but she said, "Okay—I'll only be a minute. I can take the bottle with me."

As Jonas and Eliza were walking toward the house, they were stopped twice by customers asking when they could get a buggy ride out to the barrens. Jonas assured them the buggy wagon would leave within the next five minutes. Once they were out of earshot of the second person, Eliza said, "*Ach.* I'm keeping you from your work. I don't really need a drink. I should leave so you can go serve your customers."

"I will serve them—after I've served you a cold drink," he insisted.

They reached the porch and he hopped up the stairs, went inside and promptly came out with two opened bottles of root beer.

"*Denki.*" Eliza took a sip of the beverage he handed her.

Even though he had no reason to fear she'd say no,

Jonas felt more nervous asking Eliza to go out with him now than he'd felt when he'd asked to court her the first time. His mouth was so dry he swallowed down half of his root beer. He wiped his lips with the back of his hand before speaking. "I—I was wondering if you have plans for *Sunndaag*." Without waiting for her to answer, he eagerly added, "Because if you don't, I'd like to go canoeing with you after *kurrich*. My *bruder* ate the rest of the chocolate and marshmallows, but I could buy more and we could make a campfire on the island, since we didn't get to have one last *Sunndaag*."

Eliza's smile told him everything he needed to know, even before she answered. "I'd really like that, too. But please don't get ingredients for s'mores—I'll bring a special dessert for us to share."

"Sounds *wunderbaar*," he replied. Although, if he still felt the way he was feeling now, Jonas knew he'd probably be too lovesick to eat anything on Sunday.

Chapter Nine

❦

"**W**hat's in there? Is it for lunch?" Samuel asked, pointing at the thermal bag Eliza was holding on her lap as the buggy carried their family to church on Sunday morning.

"*Neh*, it's dessert for a friend and me. We're going canoeing after *kurrich*," Eliza replied softly. She hoped Samuel wouldn't ask which friend was going canoeing with her, because she didn't want Uri to overhear and scold him for being nosy again. But the boy was more interested in her snack than in her social life.

"Is it *blohbier* muffins?" he asked.

"*Neh.*"

Isaiah took a turn guessing, too. "*Blohbier* crumble?"

"*Neh.*"

"Maybe it doesn't even have any *blohbiere* in it at all," Peter informed his younger brothers. "It might be chocolate *kuche*."

"But I didn't smell chocolate *kuche* baking last night after we went to bed. I smelled something with *blohbier* in it," Isaiah explained.

Eliza chuckled. "I can't sneak anything past your noses, can I?"

"*Neh.* My nose is awake even when my eyes are asleep," Eli said, wrinkling his nose and causing Eliza to chuckle.

Isaiah was right about what he'd smelled: Eliza had made lemon blueberry cake after the boys had gone to bed last evening. And since she couldn't justify unnecessary food preparations on the Sabbath, she'd also made hand-whipped cream to put on top of the cake, even though she would have preferred to make it fresh in the morning. Since this would have to do, she'd included the cream and cake in the thermal bag, along with two ice packs from their diesel-powered refrigerator and freezer. She hoped Jonas liked the dessert, because after the two of them had a slice, she intended for him to take the rest home.

"I'll tell you all a secret," she whispered. The boys leaned toward her so they could hear. "I made a separate *blohbier* dessert for you, too. Tonight after supper, you'll find out what kind it is."

The boys grinned appreciatively and then leaned back in their seats again. "I wish it was after supper already," Eli whispered.

"I wish I could go fishing again at the creek," Isaiah said in normal speaking volume.

"*Jah,* me, too," Peter echoed.

"I wish we could go kite flying with you, Eliza," Samuel added wistfully. "Remember you said you would take me on *Sunndaag*? Today is *Sunndaag.*"

Uri must have heard him because he scolded Samuel

from the front of the buggy. "You *buwe* need to stop pestering your *schweschder*."

They aren't pestering me, Eliza thought, but she knew it would have been rude to contradict her stepfather. So she quietly whispered to Samuel, "I will take you kite flying, but remember that I said it has to be a breezy *Sunndaag*? There isn't any breeze today at all."

In fact, the air was so still it felt stifling, and the sky was an unbroken field of white clouds. Eliza had been fretting ever since she woke that morning that it would rain and her canoeing trip with Jonas would be canceled. *Maybe if it rains he'll be willing to do something else instead*, she thought. *Even taking a buggy ride around town would be fine with me, as long as we get to spend the afternoon together.*

She was so eager to see him again that when she got to church and was seated alongside her family, she had to resist the urge to peek over her shoulder to see where he was sitting. *I'm worse than my* breider, *fidgeting like this*, she thought, as she tied a kerchief into bunny ears to keep Eli distracted during the long sermon.

After the worship service ended and Eliza was downstairs in the kitchen, helping the other women prepare lunch, Honor greeted her and Mary. "I'm rounding up people to go hiking at the gorge after lunch. So far, Glenda, Ervin, Freeman and Jacob all said *jah*. Do you two want to *kumme*?"

Secretly happy that the group was going to the gorge instead of the lake, Eliza blurted out, "It's nice of you to invite me, but I already made plans."

"Somehow, I knew you'd say that." Honor gave her a smug look. "How about you, Mary?"

"Well…*neh*. I don't think so. But *denki* for asking."

Honor's eyes went wide and she asked in a conspiratorial whisper, "Why not? Do you have *plans*, too?" She emphasized the word in a way that made it clear she really wanted to know if Mary was going out with a suitor.

"*Neh*. It's just that it looks like it's going to rain. I don't want to make the trip out there only to have to turn around," Mary said.

Her answer seemed to satisfy Honor's curiosity. She lifted two pitchers of water from the counter to carry upstairs. "Okay, but if you change your mind, we're meeting at Freeman's buggy," she said before leaving the room.

Eliza suspected the real reason Mary didn't want to go hiking had less to do with the weather than it did with the fact that Freeman would be there. On the way home from the farm on Friday afternoon, Mary had commented that she'd decided she definitely wasn't interested in him as a suitor any longer.

"Is it because he didn't apologize to you for laughing about the snake?" Eliza hadn't even waited for her friend to answer before she'd said, "Because I'm sure he will—there were just too many customers around today for him to get the chance."

But Mary had dismissively waved her hand, saying there really wasn't any need for him to apologize and she wasn't holding anything against him. She'd said she just thought his sense of humor was too different from hers. Eliza had tried to persuade her to keep an open mind, but Mary had pointedly changed the subject.

At the risk of irritating her friend now, Eliza tried one more time to get her to reconsider. "I'm surprised you're not going to the gorge," she whispered. "I thought you love it there, even when the sun's not out."

Mary hesitated and Eliza could tell she was ambivalent. "I do, but..."

"You still feel uncomfortable around Freeman?" Eliza queried and Mary nodded. "He probably feels more uncomfortable around you than you feel around him. The sooner he gets a chance to apologize to you, the sooner you'll both be able to put the incident behind you."

"*Jah*, maybe." Mary gave Eliza a little nudge from the side. "But since when are you so interested in what happens between Freeman and me?"

"Since I started praying that the Lord would provide a suitor for you," Eliza answered. *And since I've found out how much* schpass *courting can be when your suitor is someone you actually like.*

As Jonas and Eliza started out for the lake in his buggy, he was at a complete loss for words. Which was silly, considering he'd been daydreaming throughout the three-hour worship service about all the things he wanted to ask and tell her. But after church and lunch were finished and she'd come walking across the lawn toward his buggy, the sight of her sparkling smile had him completely tongue-tied.

So sitting beside her now, all he could think to ask was "Do you think the weather is going to hold until we're done canoeing?"

"I don't know. But as long as there's no lightning, I don't mind if it rains a little bit while we're out on the lake. We won't melt, right?"

"Right, we won't melt." Jonas chuckled. "That's the same thing your *breider* said when I told them to be careful not to fall in the creek. They quote you a lot, you know. It's clear they take everything you say to heart."

Now it was Eliza's turn to chuckle. She said, "*Jah*. They took what *you* said to heart last *Sunndaag*, too." She proceeded to tell him that Samuel had repeated word-for-word Jonas's justification for eating two s'mores, while the boys were only allowed one apiece.

"*Ach*. My secret's out." He momentarily covered his face with one hand. "I suppose I should have set a better example for them and waited until I got home to have seconds."

"Don't be *lappich*. You're a *wunderbaar* role model and they're still talking about all the things you taught them about fishing." Her compliment made him sit up straighter. "Besides, you couldn't help it if you were *hungerich*, considering you don't have anyone to make *appenditlich* treats for you."

Jonas's mouth watered. He'd deliberately eaten a light breakfast and he'd hardly been able to finish a bologna sandwich during the church lunch because he was so nervous about his outing with Eliza. But as he began to feel a bit more relaxed, his appetite was kicking in again. "What did you make?" he asked.

"You get three guesses," she playfully replied. "And I'll even give you a hint. It contains a yellow fruit and a—"

"You made banana cream pie? That's my favorite dessert in the world!" he interrupted, turning to watch her reaction. "How did you know?"

"Oh, *neh*?" She looked crestfallen. "If banana cream

pies is your favorite dessert, then you're going to be very disappointed in what I made. It's lemon *blohbier kuche*."

"Aha! I knew I could get you to tell me what it is." Jonas slapped his knee in amusement.

"Hey, you tricked me." Eliza bumped her shoulder against his, affectionately chiding him. "Is banana cream pie really your favorite?"

"*Neh.* In fact, the only part of banana cream pie that I actually like is the whipped cream on top."

"In that case, you'll be happy to know that I brought lots of whipped cream for our *kuche.*" Eliza abruptly clapped her palm against her forehead. "Uh-oh. I just realized I forgot to bring a spoon. Or any utensils at all."

She sounded so distraught that Jonas tried to comfort her. "We can eat the *kuche* with our hands." It wasn't uncommon for the Amish in their community to eat a slice of cake or pie with their hands, just as they'd eat a cookie, provided the cake or pie crusts were the type that held together well. The custom was just more practical than using plates and utensils, especially when they were eating outdoors or in big groups, because it saved them the effort of washing extra dishes, which they had to do by hand.

"*Jah*, that's fine, but we can't very well use our fingers to put a dollop of cream on top of the *kuche*," she lamented. "I'm sorry, Jonas. I wanted to make something you'd really like."

Touched, Jonas said, "I already *do* really like the dessert, simply because of how much care you put into making it. *Denki* for doing that for me, Eliza."

"You're *wilkom*," she replied. The note of relief in

her voice almost instantly turned to dismay as a bright white flash lit the air around them. "That was lightning I just saw, wasn't it?"

Before Jonas could answer, thunder resonated overhead, followed by a barrage of raindrops against the roof of the buggy's carriage. There was no way they could go canoeing in this weather, but Jonas had another idea. "This looks like it's just a passing shower. I know a place where we can wait it out, if you're willing?"

When she readily agreed, Jonas took a short detour, directing the horse off the main street and onto a winding side road. After about a half mile, he turned into the lot of an abandoned fuel station, bringing the animal to a halt beneath the metal canopy where the out-of-service gas pumps stood. The crumbling asphalt was littered with empty beer cans, the windows of the station were boarded up and there was graffiti scribbled across the wall.

"It's certainly not as scenic as the lake, but at least my *gaul* will be sheltered from the storm," he said.

"*Jah.* But if any *Englischers* see us here, they're going to think we're *narrish*," Eliza remarked. At first Jonas didn't know what she meant, but she explained that it might look as if they'd pulled up to the pump to get gas for their buggy. Her humorous observation made him crack up.

"Laughing like that makes my *bauch* hurt," he said, holding his stomach. "Or maybe I'm just *hungerich* for dessert."

"I am, too. I deliberately didn't eat much at lunch," Eliza admitted as she unzipped the thermal bag. "I'm glad I sliced the *kuche* already, but I really do wish I had a spoon for the topping."

"Who needs a spoon? Why can't we just dip the cake into the whipped cream?"

Eliza looked dubious, but she agreed it was worth a try. So after she'd given him a slice of cake, she opened the container of cream and extended it to him. Using his cake as a sort of scoop, Jonas pushed it through the cream, until the entire slice was slathered with it. "Are you sure you got enough?" she teased.

"I can *never* get enough whipped cream," he replied, grinning.

Then she dipped her cake into the container, too. They ate hungrily and messily, laughing about how difficult it was to take a bite of the treat without spilling the whipped cream on their clothes.

"It was definitely worth the effort, though," Jonas remarked, wiping his fingers on the napkin Eliza handed him after he finished eating his second piece. "That was *appenditlich*."

"I'm *hallich* you like it, because the rest is for you to take home."

"*Denki*. I might have to hide it before my *bruder* returns this afternoon."

"Oh, that's right. He went hiking at the gorge, didn't he?"

Even though Jonas was the one who'd mentioned Freeman, the fact that Eliza knew his whereabouts gave him pause. Narrowing his eyes, he said, "*Jah*. How did you know he was going hiking?"

"B-because Honor mentioned the outing. She asked me if I wanted to go, too." There was no mistaking that

Eliza sounded uncomfortable answering his question, and her cheeks were turning pink, too.

"Do you wish you'd gone hiking with them after all?" Jonas queried.

Eliza drew back her chin in surprise. "*Neh*, of course not. Why? Is that what *you* would have preferred to do?"

He instantly felt foolish for doubting her and terrible for making her doubt *him*. Trying to lighten the moment and reassure her at the same time, he said, "*Neh*. There's nowhere I'd rather be than here with you at this abandoned fuel station, eating *kuche* and whipped cream with our hands."

"There's nowhere else I'd rather be, either," Eliza echoed with a smile. She'd just been making small talk when she'd mentioned hiking at the gorge, so she was surprised Jonas had seemed offended by her comment. *Was he uncertain about whether she was enjoying their time together just because the date wasn't going according to plan? Or was he unsure about whether she truly wanted to be alone with him, because when he first asked to court her, she'd made a point of saying she was only interested in developing a friendship first?*

While it was true that Eliza still wanted to get to know Jonas better, she no longer considered him just a friend; she definitely thought of him as a suitor. A *real* suitor. And if he should want to hold her hand or move closer to her on the seat, she wouldn't object. In fact, she *wanted* him to. But how could she let him know that without being too forward? She turned to face him fully and said, "I like being here in the rain—it feels so cozy." She'd stopped short of using the word *romantic*, but she hoped Jonas understood it was what she'd meant.

"*Jah*, it does," he agreed, his eyes settling on her mouth. For a second, Eliza wondered if he was thinking about kissing her, but to her embarrassment, he pointed to his own lips and said, "You have a little bit of cream on your face."

She wiped her fingers across her mouth, her face burning. "Did I get it?"

"*Neh*. Here—can I?" Jonas asked and she nodded. He lifted his hand and cupped her cheek in his fingers and palm, dabbing the skin near the corner of her lip with his thumb. His touch was so gentle it made Eliza shiver. He must have thought she was trying to wiggle away from him, because he dropped his hand. "Sorry."

"*Neh*. It's okay," she said quickly. It was better than okay—it was absolutely wonderful. "You have soft hands."

He turned up his palms and inspected them. "That's because for the past couple of months I've been working on the *bauerei* instead of doing carpentry. Usually I have a lot more calluses than this," he said. For a second Eliza was sure he'd missed her hint entirely, but then he reached over and interlaced his fingers with hers. "So I'm *hallich* we started courting in the summer or I'd feel too self-conscious holding your hand for the first time."

"I wouldn't have minded," Eliza said, feeling rather self-conscious herself. On occasion, her suitors may have taken her hand to keep her from slipping on the ice or for some practical reason like that, but she'd never allowed any of them to hold her hand the way Jonas was doing now. It made her feel so breathlessly giddy,

she could hardly talk, and could barely concentrate on
what he was saying. So for the next half hour, she answered questions when he asked her, but mostly Eliza
let Jonas carry the conversation. He amused her with
stories about his family and friends in Kansas.

Finally, he said, "It doesn't look like the rain is going
to let up. I'm afraid I should probably get my *gaul* home
and wipe him down. He had a case of rain scald from
the humidity recently, so I have to be extra careful about
his skin so he doesn't get it again."

"Oh, right. You wouldn't want that happening to the
poor animal again," Eliza said, even though she was
disappointed that their date was ending already. Jonas
let go of her hand to release the buggy's parking brake
and pick up the reins, but to her delight, once they'd
pulled onto the main street, he took hold of her fingers
again. "I didn't see Emily in *kurrich* today. She must
be really sick," Eliza commented, since Amish people
only missed church when it was absolutely unavoidable.

"*Jah*. Her *mamm* told me she'd probably stay home
from work all week," Jonas replied with a sigh. "It's
going to be awfully hectic without her. After *kurrich* I
asked a couple of *meed* if they could fill in for her, but
no one is available."

"*I* could fill in for her," Eliza volunteered without
thinking twice about it.

"You?" Jonas's voice was incredulous.

Eliza pulled her hand away so she could turn sideways and look at him. "*Jah*. Why not me? I'm capable
of weighing fruit and making change."

"I have no doubts about your abilities. It's just that I

didn't realize you wanted a job," he explained. "I have to warn you, the position doesn't pay very much."

"I don't want a *job* and I don't want to get paid. I just want to help you on the *bauerei* for a few days."

"But I couldn't let you work without paying you. It wouldn't be right."

Eliza crossed her arms over her chest. "And I couldn't allow you to pay me. I have no interest in becoming your employee, Jonas. You and I are courting, and this is the kind of thing that people who—who care about each other do. I didn't pay you for babysitting my *breider* last *Sunndaag*."

"That's different. I did that to help your *familye*, not your business. And it was only for one afternoon."

"Okay, fine." Eliza shrugged, as if it didn't matter, but she actually felt a bit put out. "If you don't want my help—"

Jonas cut her off. "I *do* want your help. I would *love* your help. But are you sure your *mamm* is well enough to manage your *breider* on her own?"

Eliza honestly hadn't even considered that, but now that Jonas mentioned it, she stammered, "I—I think she should be okay."

"Well, when I swing by to pick you up, you can let me know one way or the other. How does seven thirty sound?"

"You don't need to pick me up. I walk to the *bauerei* all the time," she said.

"I know you do. But we're courting and that's the kind of thing people who care about each other do," Jonas countered, using Eliza's words against her.

He would have to get up awfully early to get all of

his chores done on the bauerei before picking her up.
It was another example of his willingness to go out of
his way for her and she couldn't refuse. "Okay," she
agreed. *"Denki."*

"You're *wilkom*." He gave her shoulder a little tap,
and when she unfolded her arms and dropped them to
her sides, he reached for one of her hands and held it
firmly all the way back to her street.

"Since your *eldre* already know that we're courting,
I might as well bring you to your door so you won't get
wet," he said as they turned in the driveway. "Unless
you don't want your *breider* to find out, too?"

"As I've said, they're too young to suspect us of
courting, so it's fine if they see you dropping me off."
Eliza giggled. "But I can't promise they won't run out
and ask why you didn't take them with you, too. They
think they're friends with you now."

Jonas chuckled. "Who knows? Maybe one day we
will take them with us."

"Maybe," Eliza said. Previously, she would have wel-
comed it if a suitor had invited her brothers to join them
on an outing because the boys would have kept the conversation from getting too personal. But today she was
in no hurry to relinquish her time alone with Jonas.

He directed his horse to the turn-around at the end
of the driveway, which was as close to the front porch
as he could get. Then he hopped out into the rain and
took her hand as she climbed out, too. *"Denki* for spending the afternoon with me. It was *wunderbaar*," he said.

"I thought so, too." She gave his fingers a quick
squeeze before reluctantly dropping his hand. "'Bye,
Jonas. I'll see you tomorrow morning."

When she went inside the house, it was unusually quiet. *The* buwe *must be napping*, she thought as she tiptoed into the living room. Her mother looked up from the letter she was writing at the desk and greeted her. Uri was seated in an arm chair, reading *The Budget*. He said hello but didn't lower the newspaper.

"Are the *buwe* asleep?" she asked.

"Eli, Mark and Samuel are," Lior answered. "Peter and Isaiah went home with the Mullet *buwe* after *kurrich*. They were supposed to try out the Mullets' new trampoline, but I'm sure they had to change their plans once it started raining."

"Oh, I don't know about that. I think the rain might make jumping on the trampoline even more *schpass* for them," Eliza said with a laugh. She was relieved that Willis Mullet's sons hadn't come *here* instead of her brothers going to their house. Otherwise, she would have been expected to join Willis and her parents for tea and dessert when he arrived to pick up his sons. This way, Uri would be going to pick up Peter and Isaiah from the Mullets' house instead.

"You came home early," he remarked, peering over the top of his newspaper. "Didn't you have a *gut* time with the Kanagy *bu*?"

"Uri," Lior said, addressing her husband under her breath. "That's Eliza's private business."

Although Eliza appreciated her mother's support and agreed it was none of Uri's business why she'd returned home early this afternoon, this was one of the rare occasions when she didn't mind telling him about her date. "Actually, we had a *wunderbaar* time. Jonas's *gaul* has suffered from rain scald recently, so he had to cut our outing short so he could go home and care for his skin. But I didn't mind, because I plan to see Jonas tomorrow, too." Eliza was nearly gloating as she explained she'd agreed to help on the farm during Emily's absence.

But Uri burst her bubble when he asked frankly, "How much is he going to pay you?"

"He—he's not," she stuttered. "He wanted to, but I'm not doing it for the money. I'm doing it because... well, because he's my suitor and I want to help him."

"That's very kind of you, Eliza," Lior said, nodding at her daughter. "I'm sure Jonas appreciates it, and working together can be a *gut* way for a *mann* and *weibsmensch* to develop a stronger relationship."

"What about helping your *mamm*?" Uri asked. "She's been ill and she still needs a lot of rest."

I'm well aware of that, Eliza wanted to retort. *But if you're so concerned about* Mamm's *health, then why don't you handle your own bookkeeping so she doesn't have to stay up late in the evenings to work on it? Or why don't you take the* buwe *outside so they're not underfoot after supper, or put them to bed in the evening?*

Instead, she quietly said, "That's true. And Jonas already knows I might not be able to *kumme* if *Mamm* is still too weak. He's going to stop by in the morning, when we'll have a better idea of how much energy she has."

"She might have energy in the morning, but that doesn't mean she'll be able to manage on her own for the entire day," Uri said, which Eliza found maddening, considering he'd been pushing her to find a full-time job. Was he just objecting to Eliza being gone for eight or nine hours because she wasn't getting paid? Or was it that he was truly concerned about Lior because he'd been sick, too, so he finally had a better understanding of how fatigued his wife was?

Lior rarely raised her voice, but now she barked, "Stop talking about me as if I'm not here, you two. And stop acting as if I'm incapable of running this household and taking care of the *kinner* by myself." She set down her writing tablet and rose to her feet. "If I'm sick or too tired to manage, then I'll send one of the *buwe* to the workshop to get *you* to help me, Uri. But Eliza is going to go assist her suitor on the *bauerei* this week and I don't want to hear another word about it."

As her mother went into the kitchen, the only word Eliza wanted to utter was *denki*. Instead, she turned and padded down the hall and up the stairs to her room, where she stretched out sideways on her bed for a nap. Pressing one hand to her cheek, she fell asleep to the pleasant sound of the rain against the roof and the memory of Jonas's touch against her skin.

Chapter Ten

Jonas got up so early to finish his chores that he actually had half an hour to spare before it was time to go pick up Eliza. He poured himself a second cup of coffee and took the remaining slice of lemon blueberry cake out onto the porch, where he sat down on a wooden glider.

Not two minutes later, Freeman came around the corner of the house. Before Jonas could say good morning, his brother pointed to the plate and asked, "What's that?"

Jonas slid the last bite of the cake into his mouth, chewed and swallowed it before answering. "Lemon blueberry *kuche*. Eliza made it."

"Is there any more?"

"*Neh.* Sorry." Jonas had eaten the rest the previous day, while Freeman was out socializing with his peers. "Didn't Honor send you home with any treats yesterday?"

"*Jah.* I was just feeding them to the *hinkel*."

Jonas chuckled. Patting his stomach, he said, "Eliza is a *wunderbaar* baker."

"*Gut*. Maybe if we drop a few hints, she'll bring extra desserts to work with her this week."

"*Jah*—for me." Jonas may not have been concerned any longer that Eliza was interested in his brother, but he did feel the need to remind Freeman of that fact. "*I'm* her suitor, not you. But there's no way we're going to suggest she should do some baking—she's already doing us a big favor by working on the *bauerei*."

His remark seemed to go right over his brother's head. "I didn't say we should *suggest* she bake something. I just said we should drop a few hints."

"*Neh*, we're not going to do that," Jonas emphatically repeated. "And you're not going to treat her like an employee or make any other demands of her, either."

"Am I allowed to talk to her at all?" Freeman retorted.

"Of course you are. But I want Eliza to know we appreciate her presence here. So be careful about what you say. You've already offended her friend—I don't want you to say something that might insult Eliza, too." Standing to leave, Jonas noticed Freeman's expression had clouded over, and he realized his brother probably still felt bad about upsetting Mary. "Sorry, Freeman. I shouldn't have rubbed that in."

"*Neh*, you're right—I do need to be more sensitive about what I say. I wish Mary would *kumme* back to the *bauerei* so I could let her know I wasn't mocking her or making light of her fears."

"Well, she said she was making jam to sell at the festival, so she's got to return soon for more *biere*," Jonas said encouragingly. "Maybe today's the day." He clapped his brother's shoulder before leaving to go hitch the horse and buggy.

As he headed toward Eliza's house, Jonas prayed that her mother would be well enough that Eliza could work on the farm. "I know it's selfish of me, Lord," he confessed aloud. "But we need her help and I really enjoy her company."

He arrived at the end of Eliza's lane to find her waiting for him there. She was holding a plastic jug in one hand and a thermal bag in the other—a promising sign. "*Guder mariye*, Eliza. What's that you're carrying?"

"Just my lunch. Why? Were you hoping it was more *kuche*?" Eliza had a twinkle in her eye as she tilted her cheek toward him. She was obviously teasing, but his reply was heartfelt.

"Well, I admit the *kuche* was *appenditlich*, but I'm even happier to know it's your lunch because that means you're able to spend the day on the *bauerei*."

"*Jah*, I am. My *mamm* feels much better this morning."

"That's great news." Jonas caught a whiff of lavender as she slid into the seat next to him. Giving her a sidelong glance, he realized it was probably her shampoo. Her hair was so shiny, she must have just washed it.

"What's wrong?" she asked and he realized she'd caught him eyeing her.

Abashed, he blurted out, "Nothing's wrong. I was just thinking about how pretty you look and how *hallich* I am to see you. I mean, not because you look pretty. I would be *hallich* to see you even if you looked *baremlich*. Not that I can imagine you ever looking *baremlich*…" The more Jonas said, the worse he sounded.

And I had the nerve to tell Freeman not to offend Eliza today, he lamented. "I just mean I really appreciate your coming to the *bauerei* today."

Eliza giggled, sounding more amused than insulted. "It's my pleasure."

"I hope you still feel that way at the end of the day. I anticipate there will be a lot of customers trying to get their picking done in preparation for the festival. Most of them are very friendly and cooperative, but I have to warn you, there are always a few demanding ones in the group as well."

"That's okay. Interacting with them will give me practice in case I get a job working with *Englischers*."

Jonas was perplexed. Hadn't she told him just yesterday that she didn't want a job? It was a minor inconsistency, but it still gave him pause. If Eliza wasn't being honest with him about her employment interests, how could he trust that she was being honest about her interest in *him*?

Giving her the benefit of the doubt, he thought, *Maybe yesterday she was just insisting she didn't want a job because she didn't want to accept payment from me.* If that was the reason, then Jonas couldn't exactly hold the little white lie against her.

Either way, he had to be sure. "I thought you told me you weren't looking for a job," he challenged.

Why did I blurt that out? Eliza silently scolded herself. *I am such a* bobbelmoul. *How am I going to explain?* She couldn't very well tell Jonas about her stepfather's demand that she either find a job or get married, because Jonas might think she was hinting that their courtship should head in that direction. And while she was growing to like him more and more every minute she spent with him, Eliza certainly wasn't anywhere near considering marriage, and she doubted he was, either.

She decided to gloss over her slip of the tongue, and said, "I'm not *looking* for a job. But you never know what the future might bring. It's *gut* to have experience dealing with different people and situations." Her explanation seemed to satisfy Jonas, who nodded, so she quickly changed the subject. "What will I be doing today besides waiting on customers?"

He described the various responsibilities of the position, then said, "You can always flag down me or Freeman if you need anything or if the customers get out of hand."

"Trust me, if I can manage my five little *breider*, I can manage this."

"I do trust you, but I'll still drop by to see if you have any questions or want to take a break or anything." Jonas added, "I usually have lunch around twelve thirty. I thought maybe you and I could both eat at the same time? Freeman can take your place waiting on the customers at the booth."

"Then who will give the *Englischers* rides in the buggy wagon?"

"No one. This morning I posted a sign saying that buggy rides won't be offered between noon and one o'clock, due to a staffing shortage."

Eliza couldn't help but smile. *He arranged all of this in advance just so we could eat together.* She was pleased he wanted to spend time with her in the middle of his working day as much as she wanted to spend time with him.

Once they reached the farm, Jonas stabled his horse, since Freeman's horse would be pulling the buggy wagon today. They'd barely made it to the booth when the first car pulled into the driveway and parked. Two young girls got out and skipped over to the booth, followed by a woman who was talking on a cell phone. Eliza had seen Emily at work often enough to know how to welcome the customers, provide them with baskets and answer their questions. Since the girls said they wanted to ride in the buggy wagon, she directed them to wait across the driveway for Freeman, who was nowhere in sight at the moment.

After the customers walked away, Jonas remarked, "Looks like you already have the hang of this. Can I bring you a cup of *kaffi* before I leave?"

Eliza couldn't recall Uri ever asking Lior if she needed anything to eat or drink, much less volunteering to bring it to her, so she was tickled by Jonas's offer. "*Denki*, but I try to limit my *kaffi* to just one cup a day... and I've already had two," she said with a giggle. "There is, however, something else I might need..."

"Anything at all. Just name it."

He leaned in expectantly, and as she watched his full, pink lips pronounce the words, Eliza thought, *A kiss. I'd like you to give me a kiss, please.* She had *never* entertained that thought about a suitor before now, and the longing was so staggering that she was sure Jonas could read it in her eyes. In fact, she *wanted* him to read it in her eyes. *Don't be* narrish. *He can't kiss you right here, in front of* Englischers *and in broad daylight*, she reminded herself.

Blinking, she cleared her throat and said, "The cashbox."

Jonas straightened up and smacked his forehead. "*Ach.* I usually bring that out and hide it on that little shelf behind the booth for Emily. But my body must have been awake before my mind was this morning, because I forgot all about it. I'll run up to the *haus* and get it."

Just as Jonas was turning to leave, Freeman came out of the house and moseyed down the porch stairs and across the lawn, holding up a brown metal box. "You missing something?" he called, and Jonas gave him the thumbs-up signal. When he was close enough that he didn't have to shout to be heard, Freeman greeted Eliza and handed her the cashbox. "It looks as if I've got customers waiting, so I'd better go. If you have any questions, just holler."

After Freeman left, Jonas said he had things to take care of on the farm, too. "Last chance to change your mind. Are you sure there's nothing else I can get you before I head out?"

Once again, Eliza was overwhelmed with the inappropriate temptation to hint that she'd like a kiss. *So this must be what romantic attraction feels like*, she marveled to herself. Aloud, she said, "*Denki*, but I have everything I need."

For now, anyway, she thought as she watched Jonas amble away. *But I still hope to receive a kiss from you. And I hope to receive it sooner rather than later...*

* * *

As much as Jonas already enjoyed working on the blueberry farm, he enjoyed it even more with Eliza working here, too. He kept finding excuses to walk by the booth, where he'd spy her counting out change for customers or helping the children tie their baskets around their waists. She always seemed to have a smile on her lips and a lilt in her voice. Jonas didn't want to disrupt her work, but he'd try to catch her eye in passing. If he did, he'd touch the brim of his hat, tipping it ever so slightly, and she'd give him a tiny nod. These brief exchanges made him feel as if they shared a secret, which put an extra spring in his step.

Jonas's only complaint was that time seemed to pass too slowly until their lunch break and too quickly during it. It felt as if they'd hardly sat down before Freeman was waving them back over to the booth because it was past one o'clock and customers were lining up at the buggy wagon. Eliza and Jonas had been so absorbed in their conversation that they'd neglected to eat, so they had to gobble down their sandwiches as they were walking across the lawn.

For the rest of the afternoon, the hours dragged by again until it was finally almost five o'clock. When Jonas approached the booth, he noticed Eliza happened to be weighing fruit for Almeda Stoll, the deacon's wife.

"*Guder nammigdaag,*" he greeted the older woman.

"Why hello, Jonas," Almeda said as Eliza handed her a bill and several coins in change. "The *biere* are really bursting with flavor this year, aren't they?"

"*Jah.* The Lord has blessed us with abundant and *appenditlich* fruit."

"Have you heard about the tropical storm coming our way on *Samschdaag* evening?" Almeda inquired. "We're only going to get the remnants of it, but the heavy rain is supposed to stick around for four or five days afterward."

Jonas winced. "That's what I heard, too. All that rain at once isn't *gut* for the *biere*—they'll go bad. But hopefully, the upcoming festival will continue to bring a lot of customers here to harvest as many ripe *biere* as possible before the storm."

"*Gott* willing," Almeda said, nodding. She turned to Eliza. "If you're done here, I can give you a ride home since your *haus* is on my way."

Jonas's shoulders drooped. He'd been waiting for hours to be able to spend time alone with Eliza again. *Please say* neh, he silently pleaded with her.

"*Denki*," she said. "But there are still customers out in the barrens, so I'll be here for a while. I don't want to keep you."

"I see." Almeda raised an eyebrow and Jonas got the sense she really *did* see what was going on, but she graciously bade them both goodbye before going on her way.

Freeman strode up to the booth from the opposite direction with a heaping basket of berries in hand. "There you are," Jonas commented. "Can you check out the last few customers when they *kumme* in from the barrens? I'm going to give Eliza a ride home."

"Now?" Eliza sounded surprised. "The *bauerei* doesn't close until five thirty." Technically, it closed at five, but there were always a few people who took their time coming in from the barrens, so it seemed as if she had fully expected to be on the farm until five thirty.

"*Jah*, but I know you need to get home to help your *mamm* make supper." He turned to his brother. "Freeman doesn't mind, do you, Freeman?"

"*Neh*, not at all. We really appreciate the work you've done for us, Eliza… Here are the *biere* I mentioned I'd pick." He thrust the basket of blueberries into her hands.

Jonas didn't know whether he was grateful for the gesture or resentful of it. On one hand, he *had* asked his brother to be especially polite to Eliza. On the other hand, Jonas wished that he would have thought of picking berries for Eliza, since that was the kind of thing a suitor should have done for the woman he was courting. Then again, throughout the day Jonas had asked Eliza if there was anything he could get for her. So why had she asked for Freeman's help, instead of Jonas's?

"*Wunderbaar*. See you tomorrow," she replied casually, and just as Jonas was pivoting to cross the driveway, he noticed that she winked at his brother. It was a brief wink, but it was undeniably a wink.

His legs felt like lead as he wordlessly trudged toward the barn with Eliza at his side. Jonas hated entertaining the kinds of suspicions that were running through his brain. *They're acting as if they have a secret. Is she going to end our courtship so Freeman can be her suitor?* Jonas couldn't ever imagine his brother betraying him like that, and he'd come to believe Eliza wasn't capable of doing such a thing, either. But he'd been blindsided before. Besides, how else could he account for what he'd just seen?

"Why are you walking so quickly, Jonas?" Eliza

asked breathlessly as she tried to match his strides. "I'd like to talk to you about something before you take me home, but I can hardly keep up with you."

Jonas slowed down. He could sense what was coming and he figured he might as well hear it now rather than on the way to her house. If she broke up with him midway, it would be awkward taking her the rest of the way home. At least if she let him know now that their courtship was over, then Freeman could give her a ride. "What is it?"

"Well, it's about your *bruder*. I'm not sure if he wants me to tell you this, but he didn't specifically say I shouldn't, so…" she began and Jonas's heart suddenly seemed as heavy as an anvil inside his chest. How could this be happening to him a third time? "Freeman picked these *biere* for Mary because he feels like it's his fault she isn't returning to the *bauerei* and he knows she wants to make a lot of jam to sell at the festival. So I told him I'd give these to her. I know it's out of our way, but I wonder if we can swing by there either this evening or first thing tomorrow morning so I can drop them off at her *haus*?"

Jonas had to refrain from throwing his hat in the air and cheering. Eliza had no intention of breaking up with him! *Why did I ever worry she was interested in Freeman?* Jonas asked himself. He was flooded with shame because he'd doubted her integrity, as well as his brother's. Yet he was also deeply relieved that he hadn't made a fool of himself by expressing his doubts.

"Of course. No problem." And as soon as they were both seated in the buggy, he finally took Eliza's hand in his, just like he'd been yearning to do ever since he'd let go of it the previous day.

Eliza was so buoyant that if Jonas hadn't held her hand all the way home, she felt as if she might have floated away. Working at his farm was even more fun than she'd expected it to be, primarily because he kept dropping by to ask how she was doing, or to bring her a bottle of root beer, or to deliver the bowl of blueberries he'd picked and washed just for her to eat as a snack.

However, upon returning home, she was dismayed to see how frazzled her mother appeared. Eliza blamed herself. *If only we hadn't stopped at Mary's* haus *to drop off the* biere, *then I would have been home to help with part of the supper preparations.* She knew they could have waited until the following morning to deliver them; the fruit would have kept. But she'd selfishly wanted to prolong the time she spent holding hands with Jonas as they rode through New Hope.

So after supper, she insisted she'd take care of clearing the table and washing and drying the dishes by herself, since she hadn't been home to help prepare supper. Now, as she scraped buttery residue from the bottom of a frying pan, she thought, *If Uri was as helpful and attentive toward* Mamm *as Jonas is toward me, she wouldn't be so run-down.* Eliza couldn't picture her suitor ever becoming as demanding as Uri seemed to be now. *If anything, Jonas has become more attentive and considerate the longer I've known him.*

"Can I, Eliza?" Samuel's imploring voice brought her back to the moment. "Please?"

"Can you what?"

"Go to the *bauerei* with you tomorrow. I can help you pick lots of *biere*."

"I won't be picking *biere*, remember? I'll be waiting on customers."

"I can help you wait on customers then. I know lots of words in *Englisch*." The Amish children in New Hope didn't formally learn *Englisch* until they started school, but they picked up words and short sentences from overhearing their parents speaking with *Englischers*.

"Okay. How would you tell a customer their *biere* cost seven dollars and forty cents?" she asked her little brother.

"I don't know *money* words," he objected. "But I can say *Englisch* food words, like *milkshake* and *cheeseburger* and *French fries*."

Tousling the boy's hair, Eliza suppressed a smile, recalling how he had learned those particular words. His older brothers had gone to a drive-thru restaurant in the buggy with Willis and his sons a year ago. Peter and Isaiah had been talking about the experience ever since. "That's excellent pronunciation, Samuel. But the only food the customers can get on the *bauerei* is *blohbiere*."

"Oh. Well, I could... I could stand in the shrubs and scare the birds away for Jonas," he insisted, wheedling her.

"That's a job for a scarecrow on a pole, not for a *bu* like you," Eliza said. She was trying to be firm, yet she was torn because she recognized how proud he'd felt that he was finally old enough to accompany her to the blueberry farm. "*Buwe* like you need to run around in big fields. It's supposed to rain this weekend, but maybe the next *Sunndaag* we can go to Hatters Field and play kickball."

"And fly kites?"

"Absolutely," she confirmed. "We might even climb trees, too—if the kites get stuck in their branches. How does that sound?"

"Gut." He was smiling again as his mother called him upstairs for bed.

However, Eliza belatedly realized that if she went kite-flying with Samuel on the Sunday after next, she wouldn't be able to go out with Jonas. The thought made her frown. But in the next moment, she recalled what Jonas had said about possibly taking the boys out with them. Her smile returned, and by the time she'd finished drying and putting away the dishes, she felt as if she might float away again.

Chapter Eleven

"Today will probably be really busy again," Jonas said as they neared the farm on Tuesday morning. "But in the future, you might want to bring your rugs with you."

"My rugs?"

"*Jah.* If there's a lull between customers, you might get bored just sitting there at the booth, so you could work on your rag rugs," he explained. "Or you could bring a book to read. Or whatever else you'd like to do."

Once again, Eliza was impressed by Jonas's thoughtfulness toward her. "*Denki,* but I've *kumme* to help. So if *you* have something else you'd like *me* to do during lulls between customers, just say the word."

"In that case…" He faced her, a sheepish, lopsided smile on his face. "I'd like you to take a break with me around ten o'clock this morning. I bought donuts on my way to your *haus.*"

There isn't a bakery on the way to my haus, Eliza thought. *He must have gotten up even earlier this morning and gone all the way into town just to have an excuse to take a* kaffi *break with me.* Usually when Eliza realized one of her suitors had schemed in order to spend more time with her, it had made her feel uncomfortable. Trapped, even. But when Jonas did it, it just made her feel special, and she wanted him to know how eager she was to spend time with him, too. "That was very thoughtful of you." Looking up at him from beneath her lashes, she coyly added, "I'll be counting the minutes."

However, the farm was so busy that Eliza lost all track of time. Both Amish and *Englisch* customers swarmed the barrens like bees on a hive. And everyone was abuzz with talk about the upcoming festival, as well as about the tropical storm that was working its way up the coast. Eliza was surrounded by so much commotion that she hadn't realized Jonas had sidled up to her, sometime after ten o'clock. Pivoting to set the fruit on the scale, she bumped into him, nearly upending the basket. He caught her arms on both sides to steady her, but his touch only made her feel more light-headed.

"I'm sorry," she whispered in *Deitsch*. "This line is growing by the minute. You'll have to take a break without me."

But Jonas insisted on staying to help until the crush of customers eased to a manageable number. Before leaving her on her own again, he joked, "We can eat our donuts at lunchtime…unless my *bruder* discovers them first."

As it turned out, there was another large influx of customers during the noon hour, with an equally large group checking out so they could go home and eat their own lunches. Meanwhile, Freeman's horse had become overheated and he needed to take the animal to the stable. So rather than sitting down to enjoy a leisurely meal and conversation, Jonas and Eliza worked side by side, which wasn't nearly as private, but was satisfying in its own way.

By five o'clock, there was still a handful of customers out in the barrens. While Eliza was waiting for Freeman and Jonas to circle around to the booth so Jonas could bring her home, an *Englisch* woman wearing high heels and a short skirt came tiptoeing across the dirt driveway.

"Oh, no," she whined when she reached the booth. "Are the berries sold out for the day?"

It took a moment for Eliza to understand what she meant. "I'm sorry, but we don't sell berries by the pint. This is a U-pick farm only."

"That's a shame," the woman replied. "There are half a dozen large businesses right down the road from here, including my employer's office. You could make a lot of money from people who enjoy fresh, locally grown produce but who don't have the time to pick it themselves. They'd appreciate being able to swing by the farm on their way home from work and grab a pint of berries."

That actually wasn't a bad idea, but Eliza knew Jonas and Freeman would have had to hire more staff members to harvest the berries, since they were too busy to do it themselves. Besides, Jonas had mentioned they didn't have the funds for additional employees. However, Eliza offered, "I could probably pick a pint or two and set them aside for you, if you'd like to return at this time tomorrow."

"Aren't you sweet!" the woman exclaimed, obviously delighted.

Eliza's motivation wasn't solely to please the customer; it was also to help Jonas and Freeman. Every pint of berries sold was one less pint that would go to waste if the weather turned bad. Eliza figured if she arrived just fifteen minutes earlier tomorrow or stayed just fifteen minutes later now, she could pick more than enough berries for the *Englisch* customer.

But when Jonas heard of her plan, he objected, saying *he* should be the one to pick the berries and that he'd do it after he'd dropped her off.

"How about if we both pick the *biere*, once Freeman gets here?" she suggested. "It'll take half as long if we're working together. And we've hardly had a chance to chat all day."

"That's true. But don't you have to hurry home to help your *mamm* with supper?" Jonas asked.

"*Neh.* As long as I do the cleanup, my *mamm* will be fine managing the preparation." At least, Eliza hoped her mother would be fine, because there was nowhere else she wanted to be right now than alone with her suitor. And as Mary had once told her, that was perfectly natural, wasn't it?

"I was *hallich* that Mary returned to the *bauerei* today," Freeman said to Jonas on Wednesday evening as they ate their supper. "I crossed paths with her out in the barrens. She seemed pleased about the *biere* Eliza gave her from me."

"*Jah*, Mary mentioned that when she ate lunch with Eliza and me, too."

"O-o-hh," Freeman uttered, nodding knowingly. "So

that's why you were glum this afternoon—you didn't get to take your lunch break alone with your girlfriend."

That was *part* of Jonas's disappointment; the other reason he was down in the mouth was because one of Emily Heiser's sisters had stopped by to tell them that Emily would be coming back to work on Friday. Of course, he was pleased about Emily's recovery, but Jonas regretted that tomorrow would be his last day working with Eliza. While it was possible she might return to the farm to pick berries for her family, that wouldn't be the same.

"I wonder if Mary plans to *kumme* to the *bauerei* tomorrow, too," Jonas muttered, not realizing he'd spoken aloud until Freeman chuckled.

"How about this... If she does, I'll ask her to have lunch with *me*. That way, you and Eliza can take your break alone together."

Jonas raised an eyebrow. "Mary might think you're interested in her romantically, you know."

"That's a risk I'm willing to take if it'll wipe that frown off your face," Freeman quipped.

Jonas couldn't tell whether his brother was sincerely being altruistic or if he was trying to disguise the fact that he truly *was* interested in Mary. Either way, he appreciated the offer, which actually did put a smile on his lips. "*Denki*. I think I'll take you up on that," he said.

"No need for thanks. Just remember this the next time Eliza bakes a dessert for you," Freeman replied, grinning as he patted his stomach.

The following morning Eliza wasn't at the end of the lane when Jonas arrived. He was so eager to see her that he got out of his buggy and paced back and forth near the fence. Through a clearing in the trees, he caught a glimpse of her hanging laundry on the clothesline, her back turned toward him. *She must have gotten up very early to have already washed and wrung the clothes*.

After she'd pinned a final pair of trousers to the line, she darted back into the house. A moment later she emerged, carrying her lunch bag. "Guess what I made yesterday evening?" she asked once they were seated side by side. Without waiting for him to answer, she said, "*Blohbier* buckle. I brought some for us to have for dessert…and a square for Freeman, too."

"*Gut*. Now I have *two* reasons to look forward to lunch—seeing you and eating *blohbier* buckle." Jonas took her hand and wiggled so close to her that their knees were touching. "I'm going to miss taking my breaks with you once Emily returns."

"*I* won't miss taking breaks together," she retorted.

He turned sideways and noticed her mischievous smirk. "You won't?"

"*Neh*," she said, nudging his knee with hers. "Because I intend to *kumme* back tomorrow."

Jonas grinned. "You're coming to the *bauerei* to pick *biere* for your *familye* tomorrow?"

"*Neh*. I'm coming to the *bauerei* to pick *biere* for *you*." In a bubbly voice, Eliza told Jonas that she'd been thinking about the customer's suggestion that they sell berries by the pint. "It seems like a *gut* idea, since the *biere* will just go to waste if they ripen and then we get so much rain that they go bad on the bushes before anyone can pick them. We could post a big sign at the end of the driveway alerting *Englisch* passersby that we're temporarily selling picked fruit, too."

Jonas found her use of the word *we* endearing; it showed how invested she was in the farm, and how connected she felt with him. However, he couldn't allow Eliza to continue working on the farm for free. "I agree that it would be *baremlich* for the *biere* to go to waste, which is why Freeman and I were already planning to pick them whenever we have spare time. We're going to ask if one of the *weibsmensch* from *kurrich* would sell them at the festival on *Samschdaag*—"

"Ooh, *jah*!" Eliza interrupted him, snapping her fingers as if something just occurred to her. "We could sell them at both places—the festival *and* the *bauerei*! I'm sure Mary would let us sell them at her booth. We could take turns managing the sales. She could attend the festival in the morning and I could attend it in the afternoon. I'll ask Uri for some pallets to transport the fruit, but we'll need to buy some pint-sized cardboard produce baskets at the farmer's exchange today after work."

"Wait a second," Jonas objected. "I don't want you to have to go through all that trouble for me and Freeman. The *bauerei* is our responsibility, not yours." Out of the corner of his eye, he noticed Eliza's shoulders slump.

"Oh. Okay," she replied in a small, quavering voice. "I was only trying to be helpful. I didn't mean to step on your toes."

Jonas slowed the horse, bringing him to a stop on the shoulder of the road. Angling sideways so he could look straight into her big brown eyes, which were brimming with tears, he touched her shoulder. "You didn't step on my toes, Eliza, and you *have* been incredibly helpful. But to continue to accept your help without giving you anything in return makes me feel like I'm taking advantage of your generosity. I don't believe that's the way people should treat each other. And it's certainly not the way a *mann* should treat the *weibsmensch* he's courting."

"I understand," she said, sniffing. "And I respect that more than you know. I really do."

But she still looked dejected, so Jonas suggested, "Maybe if I were to do something for you so your efforts didn't seem so one-sided. Is there anything you'd like me to help you accomplish?"

"Well…" Eliza tipped her head to the side, her face brightening. "You could take my *breider* kite-flying with me the *Sunndaag* after this one?"

"Pshaw." Jonas waved his hand. "I'd do that, anyway. How about something like… Like for the rest of the season, you and your *breider* can pick—or eat— all the *blohbier* you want, no charge? And whenever I can, I'll help you."

She tittered. "Talk about taking advantage of someone. You have no idea how much those *buwe* can consume! Why don't we just agree that my *breider* and I can have one morning of free picking?"

Relieved to see a smile on her lips again, Jonas countered, "*Neh*. The rest of the season or nothing. That's my final offer. Take it or leave it."

"In that case, I'll take it," she agreed.

"*Gut*. But would it be okay if you didn't tell your *breider* about our arrangement until next week?"

"Are you afraid they'll eat too many of the *biere* before the festival?"

"*Neh*." Jonas leaned toward her and openly admitted,

"I just really enjoy being alone with you. And if they're around, I wouldn't be able to do this..." He lifted his hand from her shoulder to her face. Cupping her cheek in his palm, he gazed deep into her eyes. She seemed to understand the question he was asking because she nodded ever so slightly against his hand. Or was the motion he felt only his own fingers trembling?

He paused, unsure, until her eyelids fluttered closed. Then Jonas drew closer and pressed his lips to hers for a soft, lingering kiss, the first of many they'd share during the next three days.

"But today is *Samschdaag*," Uri objected after Eliza told him where she was going. He'd been heading into the house as she was going out of it, and they'd crossed paths on the porch steps. "I didn't realize you were going to spend the afternoon at the festival."

Eliza had to hold her tongue so she wouldn't sound as impatient as she felt. Jonas was undoubtedly already waiting at the end of the lane to bring her to the festival. "I thought I told you when Jonas picked up the pallets yesterday morning."

"You didn't say anything about *you* going to the festival," Uri insisted. "Only that Jonas needed to borrow the pallets for the day."

"I'm sorry. I thought I told you," she repeated. "But I don't see what difference it makes. *Mamm* doesn't mind me going." *And you'd better get used to my not being around if I end up getting married like you've always wanted me to.* And, for the first time, like *Eliza* was beginning to want to.

Uri gruffly replied, "I was planning to surprise your

mamm by taking her out to supper. She's been running herself ragged and I thought it would be a nice change for her."

Eliza felt as if someone could have knocked her over with a feather. *Uri wants to do something thoughtful—and even* romantic—*for* Mamm? "Don't worry. I'll be home by five thirty sharp, and you can leave then. Tell her not to make anything for the *buwe.* I'll take care of fixing their meal when I get home."

After Uri grunted his agreement and went into the house, Eliza flew down the driveway to the end of the lane, where Jonas was waiting for her. Earlier that morning, Freeman had delivered the fruit to Mary's booth at the festival while Jonas managed the farm. Jonas was using his lunch break to bring Eliza to the festival, and he'd also bring her—and the pallets—home at five o'clock. Thanks to Uri, they were already a few minutes behind schedule, yet almost as soon as they pulled onto the main road, Jonas turned off onto an unpaved path. Virtually never traveled, the tree-lined dirt road was only a quarter mile long and it didn't so much come to an end as it dwindled into a grassy field.

"Why are you turning here?" Eliza asked, even though she knew exactly why he was turning here. This was the same place they'd turned for the last three days, both on the way to the farm and on the trip back so they could snuggle and kiss without being seen by passersby. "We'll be late for the festival."

"Just a few kisses," Jonas pleaded, nuzzling her ear.

"That tickles," she complained, though jokingly, as she scrunched up her shoulder. *"Absatz."*

But she only half meant it. Although she'd never been

kissed before Wednesday, now that she had, she couldn't seem to get enough of Jonas's lips on hers. She'd thought about his kisses long after she'd gotten home each evening and she'd anticipated them long before she saw him each morning. However, she also recognized that as much as she enjoyed it, there was a time and a place for kissing and it couldn't be the focus of their courtship. Rather, it *shouldn't* be. But Eliza liked this aspect of having a suitor so much that she gave in and allowed Jonas to brush his lips against hers.

"Really, Jonas," she scolded after he'd kissed her. "We need to get to the festival so Mary can go home and eat lunch. And we can't stop here on the way back, either. I promised Uri I'd return by five thirty, on the dot."

"All the more reason to give you another kiss now." Jonas proceeded to give her *three* more kisses before picking up the reins and guiding the horse back to the main road. Within fifteen minutes, they'd arrived at the fairgrounds where the festival was being held. Jonas dropped her off in the parking area, promising to return a few minutes before five o'clock so he'd have plenty of time to load the pallets into his buggy and still get her home by five thirty.

"There she is!" Mary exclaimed when Eliza arrived at her table. Half a dozen other women from their district were selling their blueberry confections, linens and crafts beneath the same tentlike canopy. "It's nearly one thirty. I thought something may have happened to you and Jonas on your way here."

Eliza could feel her cheeks going red. Even if it might have seemed logical for Jonas to give her a ride since it was his blueberries she was selling, she knew how quickly people jumped to conclusions in New Hope. In this instance, they would have been right if they assumed the pair was courting...or if Honor had already spread the rumor. But Eliza didn't appreciate her friend drawing attention to the fact she was late, probably because she already felt guilty that she and Jonas had stopped to steal a few kisses.

Before she could respond, Honor's mother, Lovina, nudged Almeda Stoll and gestured toward Eliza with her chin. "I think someone must have taken a detour," she teased. "Look how she's blushing."

Eliza wished she could have dived beneath the table. Instead, she pretended she hadn't heard and said to Mary, "You must have been very busy. It looks like most of your jam is gone already and there's not a single pie left." Over three quarters of the blueberries were gone, too.

"*Jah.* It should be slow for the rest of the day." After Mary showed Eliza which cashbox she was using for own sales and which she was using for Jonas's berries, she left. Eliza spent the afternoon chatting with the other women from her district in between sales. By four o'clock, everyone had completely sold out all of their baked goods and preserves, and they'd sold most of their embroidered products, too. One by one, their husbands or children arrived to pick them up, and although they offered Eliza a ride home, she declined, saying she had to wait for Jonas, since he was transporting the pallets back to her house.

"I could load them into the back of our buggy. We have plenty of room," Almeda's husband offered, to Eliza's dismay.

"*Neh*, Iddo. Then Jonas will have made the trip out here for nothing," Almeda interjected, winking at her. "Just be careful with those detours—they can be treacherous."

Understanding exactly what the deacon's wife meant, Eliza felt the color rise to her cheeks. But she nodded at the older woman's gentle but wise admonishment. "We're not taking any detours—I'm going straight home."

"*Gut.* Better to avoid them altogether." She smiled. "We'll see you in *kurrich* tomorrow."

Once Iddo and Almeda walked away, Eliza began stacking the pallets so they'd be easier for Jonas to bring to the buggy.

"Eh-hem." A man cleared his throat behind her.

At first she thought it was Jonas, but when Eliza spun around, she found Willis Mullet standing on the other side of the folding table. "Oh…hello, Willis."

"I see I'm too late to buy one of Mary's pies. Or a jar of her jam."

"You're too late to buy anything at all." She extended her arms, indicating the empty tent.

"*Jah.* I guess I am. Well, do you need help carrying those pallets to your buggy?"

"*Denki*, but my suitor—I mean Jonas—will be here at any moment to pick them up." Eliza averted her eyes, pretending to be embarrassed that she'd disclosed her secret, but she hadn't actually made a slip of the tongue. She had intentionally revealed that Jonas was her suitor so Willis would know she still wasn't available for courting. He didn't seem surprised, however, nor did he appear ready to leave. So she hinted, "There might be a couple of *Englischers* who are still selling goodies near the entrance to the fairgrounds. Their pies won't be as *appenditlich* as Mary's, but they might hit the spot."

Willis shifted his weight from one foot to the other. "Actually, I—I'm not that interested in pie." He leaned closer and said in a low voice, "I stopped at your *haus* and Uri told me you'd be here. I wanted to ask you something."

It ruffled Eliza's feathers to hear that her stepfather had told Willis her whereabouts, but she kept the annoyance from her voice. "What is it?"

"I—I wondered if you…" He paused for what seemed like an insufferably long time. "If you know if Mary is courting anyone?"

Willis was interested in Mary? Eliza was so astounded she couldn't speak. She just stood there, squinting at him. Eliza knew from previous conversations that her friend had absolutely no romantic interest in Willis, but how could Eliza tell him that? At one time she'd resented him for asking Uri if she'd consider courting him instead of speaking directly to Eliza about it. But now she now realized it was because Willis was shy. Or maybe he lacked confidence, since he probably hadn't courted anyone for a long time. In any case, Eliza was overcome with compassion for the widower who'd already lost so much in his life.

"Willis," she said softly, looking into his eyes. "I can't speak for Mary, but isn't she kind of…immature for you?"

"You mean young, don't you?" Willis asked. When Eliza nodded, he heaved a sigh. "*Jah*, I suppose she is."

"Have you considered courting someone closer to your own age?"

"The problem is, the only unmarried *weibsmensch* closer to my age in New Hope is Honor Bawell. And it's obvious why I could never be her suitor."

Eliza took a step backward. *What a* baremlich *thing to say. Is it just because she can't cook?* "What exactly do you mean by that?" she snapped. He must have felt ashamed because he looked down at his round stomach. So Eliza repeated her question. "Why would you say such a thing?"

"B-because, you know. Honor's so…outgoing and—and popular," he stammered. "And since she's still not married, it's clear she's very particular. She must have turned down quite a few suitors over the years. Suitors who had a lot more to offer her than I do."

Once again, Eliza was dumbfounded that she'd completely misjudged him. "You have plenty to offer a *weibsmesnch*, Willis. But the only way you'll know if Honor would agree to walk out with you is to ask her."

"I could—I could never ask to be her suitor. It would be too humiliating if…" Willis shook his head, as if imagining Honor turning him down.

"How about if you write her a note? I'll deliver it to her for you," Eliza urged him, tearing a sheet of paper off the little pad she'd been using to keep track of sales. "You can fold it up and I promise not to peek or to say a word about it to anyone."

Willis appeared dubious, but he accepted the pen and piece of paper and leaned over the table. Eliza busied herself with restacking the pallets, so he wouldn't feel as if she was hovering. When she looked up a few moments later, he was still hunched with his pen above the paper, but apparently he hadn't written anything yet. Out of the corner of her eye, she could see Jonas heading toward them.

"You'd better hurry. Jonas is coming," she warned. He scrawled his message and hastily folded the note in fours and then in fours again. He hesitated to give it to her.

"I'm not so sure about this," he said.

"It's worth a try. And I happen to think Honor would really like to be courted by you," she reassured him.

"Not as much as I'd like to court her." He pressed the little square of paper into Eliza's hand as Jonas reached the canopied area. She slipped it into her canvas bag just in the nick of time.

Jonas had seen Eliza and Willis talking from a distance, and initially, he'd thought nothing of it. But as he drew nearer, it became clear from how close they were standing that they were engaged in a very personal conversation. He'd tried not to let it bother him, but when he'd gotten even closer, he thought he'd heard Eliza tell Willis it would be an honor to be courted by him. And he was almost certain that Willis had said how much he'd like that, too. Jonas's heart had quickened as he tried to convince himself that he couldn't have heard what he thought he'd heard. *I was too far away to catch every word they said,* he'd reasoned—right until this very moment, when he'd undeniably witnessed Eliza and Willis squeeze each other's hands.

Yet even though he'd seen this with his own two eyes, Jonas knew there had to be a logical explanation.

He *wanted* there to be a logical explanation. *She just kissed me on the way to the fairgrounds this afternoon. I refuse to believe Eliza would do that and then suddenly decide she's interested in Willis instead.*

However, both Willis and Eliza appeared embarrassed when he greeted them, which did little to allay his concerns. "Do you—do you need help carrying these pallets to your buggy?" Willis stuttered.

"*Neh.* I'll manage," Jonas answered curtly, even though it would take him two trips. He bent down and lifted a stack of the pallets. Without saying anything else, he turned and carried them to his buggy. He was so appalled by what had transpired between Eliza and Willis he could hardly see straight. He could hardly *think* straight. *How could I have been so* dumm? he lamented. *This whole time, I was worried about Freeman, when it appears it's actually Willis that Eliza was trying to make envious.*

But she wouldn't do that to Jonas, would she? He resolved not to let his imagination run away with him, just because one of his former girlfriends had used Jonas to make another man jealous.

By the time he returned to the canopied area a second time, Willis was gone and Eliza was snapping the legs of the folding table flat against its underside so she easily could carry it. He picked up the remaining stack of pallets, and she accompanied him to the buggy. "Guess what? All the *biere* sold out over two hours ago!" she exclaimed as she traipsed alongside him.

"That's *gut*," he said numbly, barely hearing her blithe chatter about how big the crowd was and about how he should consider selling berries there every year. He secured the pallets in the back of his buggy, and after he climbed into the seat beside her, she handed him a small, heavy cashbox.

"This one's yours. Mary and I figured it was easier to keep the purchases separate."

"Denki." Jonas took a deep breath and began, "I noticed you and Willis seemed to be deep in conversation when I arrived..." He figured he'd give her a chance to explain before he commented that he'd also noticed she'd squeezed Willis's hand.

"Jah. He wanted to buy one of Mary's pies, but he arrived too late. They sold out even before the *biere* did. She's going to be so *hallich* that every single jar of her jam sold, too. She was worried that—"

Jonas didn't have the patience to listen to Eliza prattle on about Mary's pies or jam. He interrupted her in midsentence and bluntly asked, "What else were you and Willis discussing?"

Eliza drew back her chin in surprise. "Why are you so interested in my conversation with him?"

The very fact that she'd responded to his question with a question made Jonas even more suspicious. Yet he didn't want to come right out and accuse her of behaving flirtatiously toward Willis, so he said, "Because the two of you looked awfully...*cozy* talking together."

"Cozy?" She gave a little snortlike laugh that sparked Jonas's temper. Was this all just a joke to her? Jonas decided to cut to the chase.

"It's not funny, Eliza. You squeezed his hand. I saw you."

She made a loud, exasperated huffing sound, as if he was being ridiculous. "I did *not* squeeze his hand."

"So you're saying I was imagining it? You're honestly telling me that you two didn't deliberately touch each other's hands?"

The indignation completely melted from Eliza's expression. Apparently, she decided to take a different tack. In a patronizing voice, she said consolingly, "Our hands may have touched but not in the same way I hold hands with you, Jonas. There's no need to be envious." She reached over and squeezed his fingers but he yanked his hand away.

"I am *not* envious." Jonas's adamant tone of voice made his horse's ears twitch; he had yet to signal the animal to walk on. "You still haven't answered my question. If you have nothing to hide, you'd just tell me what you two were talking about."

She crossed her arms against her chest. "And if *you* trusted me, you wouldn't insist I tell you about a private conversation."

Jonas was so frustrated that he muttered, "I *did* trust you—which was my mistake. I should have known better than to get involved with someone who likes to string men along just for the sport of it."

"What are you talking about?" Eliza's eyes looked ready to overflow with tears, but Jonas wasn't going to allow himself to be deceived by her innocent, wounded appearance.

"Everyone in New Hope knows what kind of games you play with your suitors. You pretend to like them and just when they get serious about you, you break up with them to court someone else," Jonas retorted. "If you want to court Willis Mullet, go ahead and be my guest. I was only courting you so you wouldn't court my *bruder* and break his heart the way you did to Petrus."

Color rose in Eliza's cheeks, and her tearful expression was replaced by a steely glare. Her nostrils flaring, she snapped, "For your information, I am *not* interested in a courtship with Willis Mullet. And as of this minute, I am even *less* interested in a courtship with you, Jonas Kanagy. Or a friendship, for that matter."

"That makes two of us," he said, but she had already hopped out of the buggy and was storming across the parking lot.

Eliza saw red as she wove a path around the parked *Englisch* vehicles toward the road. She was furious at Jonas for so many reasons, she could hardly absorb them all. How dare he accuse her of stringing men along? Obviously, Petrus had told him about their courtship. Or at least, he'd told Jonas about his version of their courtship and breakup.

It's so unfair for Jonas to accuse me of breaking his friend's heart when I made it abundantly clear I only wanted a friendship with Petrus, she thought angrily. *If anyone has broken anyone's heart,* Jonas *has broken* mine. *What right does he have to act so distrustful of me? He's the one who was being deceptive. The one who was pretending to like me when his only intention in courting me was to protect his* bruder. *Which is absolutely* lecherich, *anyway.*

Eliza felt completely foolish that she'd gone to such lengths to help Jonas with his blueberry crop. And she felt absolutely disgusted that she'd allowed him to kiss her. *He has probably been laughing up his sleeve this whole time. Making a mockery of me because he thought* I *was using* him *when it was completely the other way around.*

How could she have been so gullible that she'd believed he was genuinely as considerate as he'd seemed? She should have known that kind of thoughtfulness had to be an act. *Jonas's behavior was even worse than Uri's.* But at least her stepfather was openly demanding and interfering, whereas Jonas had deliberately tried to trick Eliza into believing he was kind, appreciative and warmhearted. *I suppose I should consider it a gut thing that I found out his true colors sooner rather than later*, she told herself. Otherwise, she'd feel even more disappointed—and more infuriated—than she did now. As if that was even possible.

Trudging along the shoulder of the road, Eliza lugged the canvas bag with Mary's cashbox in it. It kept knocking against her leg, which made her feel even more miserable, and soon she was weeping. She tucked her chin to her chest so passersby wouldn't see that she was crying.

Hot, sticky and both emotionally and physically drained, Eliza arrived home more than an hour later to find Uri sitting in a glider on the porch. "You promised you'd be home at five thirty so I could go out with your mother," he reminded her. "It's almost six thirty now."

Eliza paused on the top step. Couldn't Uri see how upset she was? For all he knew, she'd been in a buggy accident. Couldn't her stepfather have at least inquired about her welfare before lecturing her about being late? Without looking at him or offering an explanation, she said, "I'm sorry. I'll fix the *buwe's* supper as soon as I wash my hands. You and *Mamm* can leave whenever you're ready."

"There's no point to it now—your *mamm* heated up stew for all of us."

Eliza took another step closer to the door, but Uri wasn't finished with his lecture. "You've been spending entirely too much time with your suitor lately and neglecting your responsibilities here. It's not acceptable."

Clenching her hands into fists at her sides, Eliza refrained from saying, *Nothing I ever do is acceptable to you. When I don't have a suitor, you lecture me about getting one. When I am courting, you complain I'm not home often enough. There's just no pleasing you.*

Instead, she said, "I promise it won't happen again." And as she yanked the door open, she added silently, *Because I'm not courting anyone for the rest of my life.*

Chapter Twelve

~❧~

Eliza woke on Sunday morning, still dressed in the clothes she was wearing on Saturday evening when she'd dropped onto her bed, crying. She must have been more tired than she'd realized.

Closing her eyes again, she listened to the heavy rain hitting the roof, which reminded her of sitting in Jonas's buggy with him at the deserted gas station. She groaned and shifted into a sitting position, banishing the memory from her mind. There was no sense in starting today as miserably as she'd ended yesterday.

I've shed enough tears over Jonas, she told herself when she saw her puffy eyelids in the bathroom mirror. *I'm not going to waste another minute thinking about him.*

After washing her face, brushing her hair and changing into fresh clothing, she headed downstairs. As much as possible, Eliza and her mother didn't cook on the Sabbath, so breakfast on Sunday usually consisted of little more than toast and boiled eggs. In the kitchen, her mother was already laying the bread on a cookie sheet to slide into the oven, which was how the Amish toasted their bread.

"Guder mariye," Eliza cheerfully greeted her, hoping Lior wouldn't notice that her eyes were pink-rimmed. Before retreating to her room the evening before, Eliza had managed to compose herself long enough to apologize to her mother for ruining her plans with Uri. But she hadn't explained *why* she'd returned home later than she'd said she would, and she didn't want to elaborate on it now, either. "What can I do to help?" she asked.

"Could you please get another jar of jam from the basement? The *buwe* have nearly polished off this one already." Lior scraped a spoon against the bottom of the jar. "I hope you plan to go picking for us this week, now that the festival is over?"

"Neh." Eliza's answer sounded too brusque, even to her own ears, so she added, "It's supposed to rain."

"Jah, but only through *Mittwoch.* Then the skies should be clear for the rest of the week. I'm sure the *buwe* will be *hallich* to help you…if you don't mind taking them along, that is."

"Mmm," Eliza responded vaguely and scurried from the room. As she went downstairs to retrieve a fresh jar of jam, she recalled Jonas's offer for her and her brothers to pick as many blueberries as they wanted, without charge. It added insult to injury that she'd toiled for a full week for the benefit of his farm, yet he was getting out of holding up his end of the bargain.

I have half a mind to show up with the buwe *to pick* biere *from eight in the morning until five at night every sunny day from now until the season ends*, she thought. But what would be the point in that? All the free blueberries in the world wouldn't be enough to make up for how he'd treated her. How he'd *tricked* her. Besides, being around Jonas would only make her *think* about Jonas, and thinking about Jonas would only make her mad. Or sad. *And I've already cried enough over him*, she reminded herself again as she brought the jam back upstairs.

After the family had eaten breakfast and held their home-worship service, Eliza's brothers quietly drew pictures and played with their blocks while the adults read the Bible to themselves. Then Eliza and Lior made sandwiches for lunch. "Uri and I are taking the *buwe* to the Mullets' *haus* this afternoon. Lovina Bawell's *kinskinner* are visiting so she's bringing them over, too."

"That's a lot of *kinner* in one *haus* on a rainy afternoon."

"*Jah.* But Willis has that large basement where they can play while the *eldre* are visiting upstairs," Lior replied. "You're *wilkom* to *kumme* with us, but I imagine you have plans?"

"Mmm." Once again, Eliza didn't directly answer her mother's question. She figured that even though Willis hoped to court Honor, there was no guarantee she'd say yes, and if Uri found out Eliza and Jonas had broken up, he might still try to push Eliza and Willis together.

However, Eliza was struck with an idea about how she might help hasten Willis and Honor's courtship along. So before her family set out for the Mullets' house, Eliza wrote a note to Honor indicating Willis had asked her to pass along the enclosed message. Then she put both pieces of paper in a sealed envelope and gave it to her mother to give to Lovina, so she in turn could pass it to Honor.

Please, Gott, *if it's Your will, let Honor give Willis a chance*, she prayed silently as she watched Uri's buggy pull through the deep puddles on the driveway before turning down the lane. Eliza's intention in making this request to the Lord wasn't primarily because she wanted to eliminate the possibility that her stepfather would cajole her into courting Willis. It was that she truly wanted her friend to have the desire of her heart. *I just hope her heart doesn't wind up broken, like mine did*, Eliza thought bitterly.

This was the first time in ages that she'd been alone in the house for an entire afternoon and she felt at a loss for how to occupy her time. If the weather had been better, she would have walked to Mary's house, but the rain was coming down in sheets. So Eliza decided to read a novel she'd checked out of the library so long ago she'd forgotten which character was which and she had to start reading it from the beginning again.

As hard as she tried to focus on the storyline, intrusive thoughts about Jonas kept interfering. *I can't believe he'd think I'd kiss him in one moment and then break up with him in the next just so I could court Willis*, she grumbled to herself. *He's as mistaken about* my *character as* I *was about his. He sure had me fooled about what a* wunderbaar mann *he was!*

Just as tears threatened to spill, Eliza heard footsteps on the porch. For a split second, she thought, *It's Jonas—he's* kumme *to apologize.* She rose and went to answer the door, pausing before she opened it to pull back her shoulders and hold her chin high. She didn't want him to get the impression she'd been wallowing in sorrow.

But instead of Jonas, she found Mary on the porch, which made her feel both disappointed and relieved at once. "Hi, Mary. Am I ever *hallich* to see you. *Kumme* in," she urged and her friend closed her umbrella and stepped indoors. "It's raining buckets out there—how did you ever manage to stay so dry walking all the way from your *haus*?"

"I didn't walk. I got a ride." Mary hesitated, glancing over Eliza's shoulder before she whispered, "Can I talk to you in private?"

"Don't worry, we're the only ones here. *Kumme* sit in the kitchen. I'll make tea."

"*Denki*, but I can't stay," Mary replied in a normal volume. She gave Eliza a shy smile, then blurted out, "Freeman is waiting for me at the end of your driveway. Yesterday morning when he dropped off the *biere* at the festival, he asked me to walk out with him!"

"He did? How *wunderbaar*!" Eliza exclaimed, genuinely happy for her friend. *I only hope Freeman treats you better than his* bruder *treated me.*

"That's why I may have seemed impatient when you showed up late to the festival yesterday—I was dying to tell you. But there were so many *weibsleit* from *kurrich* nearby that I ended up keeping it to myself, because I didn't want them to hear," Mary explained. "Freeman doesn't know I'm confiding in you about it, though. I made an excuse to stop here. I told him I needed to pick up my cashbox, which I actually do since I'd like to deposit my earnings in the bank tomorrow."

"*Schmaert* thinking. I'll go get it." Eliza dashed up

to her room and returned a moment later with the box, which she extended to her friend.

As Mary accepted it, she said, "*Denki* for this. And *denki* for praying that I'd meet a suitor. I'm really *hallich* you convinced me to give Freeman a second chance."

"You're *wilkom*." Eliza frowned, thinking about how she wished she'd never given Jonas a *first* chance.

Mary must have noticed her expression because she asked, "Is something wrong?"

"I just…never mind. I'll tell you about it later." She didn't want to delay her friend's outing with Freeman.

"But I feel guilty leaving you all alone, knowing something's troubling you."

"Well, you shouldn't. It's perfectly natural for you to be excited about spending time alone with your suitor," she insisted, quoting what Mary herself had previously said. "Go have *schpass*. I'll be fine."

But as soon as she'd closed the door, Eliza crumpled into a heap on the sofa and wept herself to sleep.

On Saturday during supper, Jonas poked his fork into a small square of ham, but instead of lifting it to his mouth, he mindlessly pushed it around in circles on his plate. Ever since he'd broken up with Eliza, he'd had a bitter taste in his mouth and a churning feeling in his stomach that had made it nearly impossible for him to eat.

Jonas had tried to tell himself that this physical response to their breakup wasn't because he was sad—it was because he was *angry.* He was angry at Eliza for denying that she was interested in Willis, even after he'd caught her cozying up to him and directly confronted her about it. But he was even angrier at himself for becoming romantically involved with her despite his better judgment.

As he'd done countless times during the last week, he silently berated himself for losing sight of the very reason he'd started to court her in the first place—to keep her from playing games with his brother's heart. Instead, she had played games with *Jonas's* heart. And deep down, beneath all his anger, he had to admit how much it hurt to discover she'd just been toying with him. *It serves me right for being so* dumm. *I knew better than to allow myself to get close to another* weibsmensch. *Especially one like Eliza.*

"If you don't finish your supper, you won't get any dessert," Freeman joked, interrupting his thoughts. "And you'll definitely want dessert tonight—it's pie that Mary baked."

Jonas's brother had confided that he'd asked to be Mary's suitor the previous weekend, and she'd said yes. She'd come to pick blueberries on Thursday and Friday mornings, once the rain finally stopped, and the couple had eaten their lunches together on both days. Freeman had taken her out yesterday evening, too. He seemed happier than he'd been in years. In fact, he seemed every bit as happy as Jonas was *un*happy.

"No pie for me, *denki*. I'm not very *hungerich*," he said with a sigh.

Freeman narrowed his eyes, scrutinizing him. "Why are you so glum? Is it because Eliza wasn't able to *kumme* to the *bauerei* this week? You should have taken her out one evening after work. I know you've been concerned about your *gaul* getting rain scald again, but the weather was dry last night. And the night before."

Jonas avoided the topic of Eliza, and simply answered, "My *gaul's* skin is completely healed now."

"Then why have you been moping around ever since the blueberry festival? Did you and Eliza have an argument?"

"That's none of your business," Jonas barked. Then he dropped his fork onto his plate and leaned back in his chair in resignation. "But since you're going to find out through the grapevine soon enough, anyway, I might as well tell you. We're not courting anymore. She's interested in someone else."

"Wow." Freeman set down his utensils, too. Shaking his head, he added, "I'm really sorry to hear that. I've been praying that your relationship would continue to grow deeper."

"You have?" Jonas was moved that his brother had such a magnanimous attitude toward him, considering Freeman was interested in becoming Eliza's suitor before Jonas began courting her.

"*Jah.* I know you've been…well, disappointed by relationships in the past, but you seemed really joyful while you were courting Eliza. And she's so different from the other *weibsleit* you've courted that I was hoping your relationship would last for the long haul." He chuckled ruefully. "And for the short term, I also thought it would be a lot of *schpass* if you and Eliza and Mary and I raced canoes at the lake together tomorrow afternoon."

Maybe you and Mary can go canoeing with Willis and Eliza instead, Jonas thought bitterly as he rose to bring his plate to the sink. "If you're going to the lake, I assume that means we'll be riding to *kurrich* in separate buggies?"

"Jah." Freeman got up to remove a large glass container from the fridge. "You sure you don't want pie?"

Jonas shook his head. "I'm going to go take a shower," he said before lumbering down the hall. But instead of ducking into the bathroom, he continued to his room, where he dropped onto his bed with a moan. Knowing what he knew from his previous breakups, he anticipated that even catching a glimpse of Eliza in church tomorrow was going to be an awkward, uncomfortable experience. It would undoubtedly trigger all sorts of uncharitable thoughts and feelings that Jonas was aware were displeasing to the Lord. It was bad enough that he'd been wrestling with those emotions all week, but somehow it seemed even worse to be troubled by them during worship services.

Although he recognized he ought to ask the Lord for a more forgiving attitude, Jonas's anger was still smoldering deep within his heart. Quite frankly, he wasn't ready to even *want* to forgive Eliza yet. Besides, he was exhausted. So instead of praying, he rolled over, closed his eyes and went to sleep.

After she'd helped her mother get the boys into bed, Eliza sat down at the folding table in the living room, where she'd been braiding rugs every spare moment she had this week. *I'll be able to take these to Millers' Restaurant on* Muundaag *for consignment*, she thought as she surveyed her handiwork. *This has been a much better use of my time than working on Jonas's* bauerei *for free.*

As much as she'd been trying not to think about him, Jonas kept creeping into her mind. She shook her head, as if to clear her brain of him. "I think it's supposed to be breezy out tomorrow," she commented to her mother, who was sipping tea on the sofa beside Uri as he read *The Budget.* "I'd like to take the *buwe* kite flying at Hatters Field after we return from *kurrich*, as long as you don't mind if I use the buggy."

"*Neh.* That's fine. It would be a treat to *kumme* home and take a nap in peace, wouldn't it, Uri?" Lior nudged her husband.

He lowered his newspaper and peered at Eliza. "Don't you have plans to go out with the Kanagy *bu* tomorrow?"

Her stepfather's nosy question instantly riled Eliza. *He's not a* bu, *he's a* mann *and his name is Jonas. But, neh, I'm not going out with him ever again.* Instead of voicing her response aloud, she merely shook her head and began twisting a length of fabric for the new rug she was beginning.

"You haven't seen him for quite a while," Uri remarked. Eliza knew this statement was really meant to be a question; it was his way of asking *why* she hadn't seen Jonas lately. As usual, she didn't think the details of her social life were any of Uri's business, so Eliza just shrugged without looking up. But Uri didn't take her silence as a hint that she didn't want to discuss the matter with him. He persisted, and asked, "When do you think you'll go out with him again?"

Maybe it was because she was worn out from struggling to work through her anger and sadness all week, but Eliza could no longer seem to hold her tongue. "Never. I am *never* going out with Jonas Kanagy again," she declared, jumping to her feet. "I'm not going out with *any* suitor ever again. So if you want me to move out of the *haus*, I'll move out. But I'm not going to court someone and get married just so *you* can have a partner to help you run your workshop."

Eliza turned and fled to her room before either her mother or stepfather could reply. She must have sobbed into her pillow for fifteen or twenty minutes before there was a knock on the door. Eliza invited her mother to enter, but she didn't sit up or turn around. She anticipated Lior crossing the room to sit beside her on the bed, but her mother kept her distance. She didn't speak, either, so Eliza began the conversation.

"I'm sorry if I sounded disrespectful, *Mamm*, but I can't tolerate the way Uri interferes in my private matters anymore. My courtships—or lack of courtships— are none of his business."

She heard a cough, and in the next instant Eliza realized she'd made a mistake; it wasn't her mother who was standing in the doorway, but Uri. "You're right. Your courtships *aren't* any of my business—that's a point your *mamm* has repeatedly tried to drill into my thick noggin. However, I've been a slow learner," Uri said. Eliza was so stunned to discover it was her stepfather, not her mother, in the doorway that she couldn't reply. But she was even more astounded when he actually apologized to her. "I'm sorry for prying."

Eliza rolled over and sat up, placing her feet on the floor. Too embarrassed to meet his eyes, she looked down at her knees and nodded, indicating she had accepted her stepfather's apology. But he wasn't done explaining.

"I realize I've pushed you into courtships. And you're right, it's been because I've wanted a *mann* in the *familye* who could run the business in the event that—that something happens to me." Uri pulled on his beard. "I'm not a spring *hinkel* anymore, you know."

Although Eliza realized he was trying to lighten the mood, her eyes teared up. *He's been worried about who would provide for our* familye *if he became ill or died,* she realized. *That's probably why he wanted me to get a full-time job, too—so I could provide an income if* Mamm *and the* buwe *needed one.*

Her stepfather continued, "However, your *mamm* has been reminding me that I don't know what the future holds, but *Gott* does. And He will provide for our *familye*, no matter what… That's why Lior and I decided last week that rather than increase the number of my employees, I'm going to decrease the number of orders I accept. At least until the *buwe* are older and they can help in the workshop."

"That sounds like a *gut* plan," Eliza murmured.

"*Jah*—and I have your *mamm* to thank for coming up with it." Uri paused, a contemplative look on his face, and it occurred to Eliza how much he seemed to respect Lior's quiet but persistent advice. "So that's why I was asking when you were going to see Jonas again—I need him to return the pallets he borrowed. As long as they aren't stained from the *blohbiere*, I can include them as part of an upcoming order."

"Oh, I see," Eliza quietly replied. "Do you suppose

you could ask him for them after *kurrich* tomorrow? We're not exactly on speaking terms right now."

"I'm sorry to hear that," Uri replied, shaking his head. "I really thought he was a *gut* match for you. I had high hopes that this courtship might even result in marriage."

Exasperated that her stepfather was already slipping into his old habits again, Eliza protested, "But you just said—"

Uri cut her off. "I didn't want you to continue to court him for *my* sake or for the sake of the business. I hoped you'd continue to court him because you've never seemed so *hallich* about spending time with one of your suitors as you did with him."

That's because I never fell for one of my suitors before, Eliza thought. And she'd never fall for another one again, because she never wanted to *have* another suitor again. Nor would she need to, now that Uri had decided not to pressure her into a courtship. The thought should have made her feel comforted, but as she followed her stepfather back downstairs to have a piece of blueberry cheesecake, Eliza could barely hold back her tears.

After lunch—he'd barely eaten half a sandwich— Jonas was one of the first men to reach the hitching rail on Sunday. Seeing Eliza sitting two rows up from him had made him want to flee ever since he'd first arrived at church three and a half hours earlier. Especially since he'd noticed Willis Mullet and his sons were sharing the pew with her family.

Jonas had almost finished hitching his horse and buggy when he realized he'd forgotten his Bible inside, so he had to go back in to look for it. He'd gotten side-tracked by Iddo Stoll, who'd engaged him in a fifteen-minute conversation. By the time Jonas had retrieved his Bible, there were only a few buggies still hitched to the post...and to his dismay, Honor Bawell was waiting next to his.

"*Guder mariye,* Jonas," she said gaily. "Have you seen Eliza? I can't find her and I was sure she'd be with you."

"What makes you think that?" Jonas asked.

"Oopsie. I guess she didn't tell you I found out that you're courting." She giggled. "Don't worry, I haven't told anyone, even though I'll personally never understand why some people are so secretive about who they're courting."

Jonas didn't feel like telling Honor, of all people, that not only was he *not* courting Eliza, but they also weren't even on speaking terms any longer. "I think Eliza already left," he said flatly. "In any case, she's not with me."

"That's too bad." Honor winked at him as if she assumed he was going to meet up with Eliza later but was pretending he wasn't for the sake of privacy. "But if you happen to see her, could you please tell her I said *denki* for encouraging Willis to ask if he could be my suitor?"

Jonas inhaled sharply. "Willis is courting *you*?" he clarified, barely able to keep the incredulity out of his voice.

"Don't sound so surprised!" Honor stuck out her bottom lip.

Jonas rushed to apologize. "*Neh,* I didn't mean it like that. I just thought that Willis was..." He stopped short, unable to explain why he was so baffled. Thankfully, Honor jumped to her own conclusions about what he'd meant.

"I know. I thought the same thing—Willis is so shy." Honor beamed. "And he is, too. If Eliza hadn't suggested he write me a note, he probably never would have asked me to walk out with him. So be sure to tell her I said *denki*."

As Honor turned and practically skipped toward Willis's buggy, Jonas felt as if the earth was spinning. *Was that what Eliza had been speaking to Willis about at the festival?* he wondered. If it was, then Jonas could understand why she had refused to tell him the details of their conversation.

His mind reeling, he pulled himself into his buggy. But instead of picking up the reins, he covered his face with his arm, blocking out the bright sunlight. Yet he couldn't block out the realization that he had wrongly accused Eliza of being a game player.

His stomach felt like it was turning somersaults as he recalling how baffled—how *hurt*—she'd appeared when he'd said that everyone knew she strung men along for sport. Even if that had been Petrus's perception of his experience courting Eliza, it hadn't been Jonas's experience. He'd had no right to accuse her of such behavior. Even worse, he'd wrongly accused her of flirting with Willis. Of being romantically interested in him. *I essentially called her a liar*, he realized, mortified.

Jonas picked up the reins and signaled his horse to walk on. There was absolutely no reason he should expect Eliza to accept his apology. But that didn't mean he wasn't going to beg her forgiveness.

* * *

"Look at how high my kite is, Eliza!" Samuel exclaimed, releasing one hand from the spool to point to the sky.

"Hold on tight with both hands or you'll lose it," she warned.

"Okay. I will," the child promised as he slowly walked closer to where Peter and Isaiah were flying their own kites.

As it happened, both Eli and Mark had fallen asleep on the way home from church, so Eliza had only taken the three eldest boys to Hatters Field. They couldn't have been more delighted, and she tried to match their enthusiasm about the activity, but her mind drifted back to the pastor's sermon today. He'd read the third chapter of Colossians and Eliza was struck by the thirteenth verse, which urged believers to forbear and forgive one another, just as Christ had done for them.

I suppose I could forgive Jonas for thinking I was flirting with Willis, she reasoned. After all, it probably had looked like they'd been holding hands and Eliza was very secretive about their discussion. But she didn't know how she would ever forgive Jonas for using her. *I don't care if Petrus may have told him, it wasn't right for Jonas to kiss me if he didn't truly like me. It wasn't fair for him to let me think we had a romantic future together. I never misled any of my suitors like that. I didn't even hold their hands.*

Noticing her brother's string was going slack as the breeze let up, Eliza called to him, "Wind it tighter, Samuel!" But it was too late—the kite dropped to the ground in the distance. As he was running to retrieve it, Eliza noticed movement in the corner of her eye. "Uri? What are you doing here? Is *Mamm* okay?"

"*Jah.* She's still napping and so are Eli and Mark. I decided I wanted to fly kites with the *buwe.*"

"You walked all this way from the *haus*?"

"*Neh.* I..." He paused, adjusting his hat. "I got a ride from Jonas."

"Oh." Eliza figured Uri must have asked him to drop off the pallets he had borrowed. "I'm surprised he delivered the pallets on the *Sabbaat.*"

"He didn't. He came to our *haus* looking for you. He's waiting for you in the parking area over there." Uri pointed to a row of trees at the edge of the field. "At the risk of interfering in your personal business, I agreed to give you the message that he'd like to speak with you. But if you want me to tell him to go away, I will. No questions asked."

Eliza glanced in the direction her stepfather was pointing and then looked across the field to where Isaiah and Peter's kites, like Samuel's, had also dropped from the sky. It appeared they were trying to unsnarl a web of strings on the ground. *I suppose talking to Jonas might be a* little *easier than trying to help the* buwe *untangle their kites*, she thought. Sighing, she said, "I'll be back in a few minutes."

When she rounded the stand of trees near the parking area, she spotted Jonas's buggy before she spotted him. He was leaning against a split-rail fence about twenty yards away, his head bowed and his hands clasped across his stomach. Was he praying? He couldn't possibly be *crying,* could he?

As she neared him, he lifted his head and Eliza immediately noticed how pale he appeared. Even the green of his eyes seemed to have faded. Her concern for his physical well-being momentarily overshadowed her anger and she blurted out, "What's wrong? Are you sick?"

"Jah." He straightened his posture and came toward her, his mouth flattened into a tight, grim line. "I'm sick about the way I treated you, Eliza. I'm so sorry I accused you of flirting with Willis. I know you're not interested in him."

Now that she knew he wasn't actually physically ill, Eliza took a step backward and crossed her arms over her chest. She wasn't ready to forgive him. "What made you change your mind all of a sudden?"

Jonas licked his lips before answering. Either he was very nervous or very thirsty. Maybe both. "Honor asked me to thank you for encouraging Willis to ask her to walk out with him."

Inwardly, Eliza smiled, in spite of herself. *That means she accepted him as her suitor*, she thought, pleased on her friend's behalf. But outwardly, she was frowning. Since Honor had apparently let the cat out of the bag already about her courtship, Eliza explained, "*Jah*, that's what Willis and I were talking about at the *blohbier* festival. He was giving me a note to pass to her." She sighed and then admitted, "I suppose it probably did look like we were holding hands, though, so I understand why you may have been suspicious. But it hurt my feelings that you didn't believe me when I specifically told you I wasn't interested in Willis. I was angry that you didn't trust me more than that."

Jonas nodded. "You're right, I should have believed

you. But my lack of trust wasn't a reflection on *your* character. It was a reflection on mine." Jonas removed his hat and fanned himself before putting it back on his head. He asked if Eliza minded moving out of the sun, and he seemed so shaky that she followed him farther down the fence to a shady spot beneath the tall pines. They both leaned against the rail and looked toward the trees instead of at each other.

After a long pause, Jonas said, "I've been betrayed in two courtships. One of the *weibsleit* only courted me to make someone else jealous. The other one…well, she didn't really have any genuine interest in me as a suitor—she just didn't want to be single. Both times I was crushed to find out that—that I'd been used." Jonas rubbed his jaw and shifted to face Eliza. "After the second breakup, I felt like I just couldn't trust *weibsleit* anymore. In retrospect, I realize how much unforgiveness I've been harboring in my heart and how unfair my attitude toward *weibsmensch* has been…especially toward you. And I'm very sorry."

Although she appreciated what Jonas had shared about his past and she could see how it had contributed to his recent behavior, Eliza still needed to have her say before she could accept his apology. "I understand why your previous experiences as a suitor may have affected your outlook on courting. And I can see why you might have thought you were protecting your *bruder*. But for the record, I've never strung any suitor along just for the sport of it. And that includes Petrus, regardless of whatever he may have told you. In fact, I've always made it clear to every suitor I've ever had that I only wanted to start with a friendship."

Out of the corner of her eye, she could see Jonas's head moving up and down. "I remember you saying that same thing to me, too. You were very straightforward. I'm the one who was untrustworthy and deceptive for entering into a courtship with you, knowing full well I wanted to remain single for the rest of my life."

Eliza inhaled sharply at Jonas's words. It was as if she'd just looked into a mirror of her own behavior and was appalled by what was reflected there. She swiveled her head to meet his eyes and confessed to herself as much as to him, "I've entered courtships under false pretenses, too."

Jonas furrowed his brow. "What?"

"The only reason I ever walked out with anyone was because Uri had been pressuring me to have a suitor, not because I was interested in a courtship. And not because I ever wanted to get married." The words seemed to fly from Eliza's mouth as she blinked back tears of shame and regret. "I thought that because I was so careful to tell my suitors that there was no guarantee we'd have a romantic relationship, then I wasn't being dishonest. But I was really being every bit as deceptive as—" She stopped herself in midsentence.

Jonas finished it for her. "As *I* was?" His face turned red and he snorted. "*Ha.* You were a lot *more* deceptive than I ever was."

Eliza could understand how angry and disappointed he must have felt to discover she'd only pretended to be interested in having a suitor when he'd first asked her to walk out with him. But she didn't think it was fair for Jonas to heap more blame on her when she was trying to apologize. Especially in light of his own transgressions. "What makes you think my behavior was any worse than yours?" she demanded.

"Because you held my hand. You kissed me!" he said in a loud voice.

"You held *my* hand and you kissed *me,* too!" she echoed, equally loud.

"*Jah*, but by that time, I sincerely liked you. By that time, I had reconsidered staying single for the rest of my life." Jonas snickered in disgust. "I never would have kissed you otherwise."

"Well, by that time *I* really liked you, too!" Eliza realized she was actually shouting, so she lowered her volume and crossed her arms against her chest. "And for your information, you're the only suitor I've ever kissed. The only suitor I ever held hands with, for that matter. Because you're the only suitor I ever developed any romantic feelings for."

"Oh."

"*Jah*. Oh," Eliza said as she sullenly mimicked him. She turned to face straight forward again, absently watching a chipmunk scampering beneath the trees as she reflected on what she and Jonas had just admitted to each other.

After a few moments of shared silence, he sidled closer to her and brushed her prayer *kapp* string over her shoulder, causing her to shiver. "Do you *still* have romantic feelings for me?" he whispered into her ear.

"Not at the moment, *neh*," she claimed, shaking her head, but she was only teasing. However, her tone grew serious when she asked, "Do you forgive me for deceiving you?"

"Jah." Jonas's voice was solemn, too. "Do you forgive me?"

"Jah."

Eliza was silent again for another minute, as the sweetness of their reconciliation washed over her. Then Jonas nuzzled her ear once more. *"Now* do you have romantic feelings for me?"

After stealing a look around to be sure no one else was in the area, she turned her head toward him, and when she nodded, their noses bumped.

You're not just the only mann *I've ever kissed*, Eliza thought as their lips met. *You're the only* mann *I ever want to kiss...*

Epilogue

"Look at this," Samuel said to Jonas, pointing to the ragged green leaves. After courting for over a year, Eliza and Jonas were getting married in two weeks. Since Jonas's extended family and several of his friends were coming from Kansas to attend the ceremony, Eliza wanted to be sure they had plenty of the leafy green vegetable for their wedding meal. So she, Lior and Uri had cultivated a celery patch that was almost as large as the rest of their garden. But rabbits had been snacking on the celery, much to Samuel's dismay. "Do you know what kind of rabbit ate these leaves?" he asked.

"Cottontails? Or snowshoe hares?" Jonas mused. When the child shook his head, Jonas asked, "Then what kind of rabbit do you think it was?"

"The *hungerich* kind!" Samuel exclaimed, making Jonas laugh as hard as he'd laughed the first time the child had made the same joke about the birds eating blueberries at the farm.

"Speaking of *hungerich*, your *breider* are in the *haus* eating pumpkin *kuchen* with your *daed* and *mamm*,"

Eliza said. "You should go join them before all the treats are gone."

"Okay. 'Bye, Jonas. 'Bye, Eliza." Samuel skittered into the *haus* and Eliza and Jonas climbed into his buggy. As soon as they were seated next to each other, he took her fingers in his.

"Remember that day we ate *kuche* and whipped cream without forks in your buggy in the rain?" Eliza asked, reminiscing. "On the way home, you held my hand for the first time. I was so distracted by your touch I could hardly concentrate on anything you were saying."

"You think *you* were distracted—imagine how I felt. I had to hold your hand, talk and guide the horse all at the same time. It's amazing we didn't end up in a ditch."

"It still makes my heart skip a beat every time you take my hand."

"And it still nearly makes me go off the road," Jonas said, turning his head to smile at her.

When they arrived at the Hiltys' property a few minutes later, Mary, Freeman, Honor and Willis were already there, donning life vests by the water's edge.

"Let's race to Pine Island," Freeman suggested. "My fiancée and I will take this canoe."

"My *husband* and I will take the other one," Honor said. Because Willis had already been married, he wasn't required to wait until the fall wedding season to wed, so he'd married Honor the previous April. During the past six months of marriage, he'd lost over thirty pounds. Almost everyone in the district credited Honor's cooking for his weight loss, but Honor had boasted to her friends that Willis claimed he was too happy to overeat any longer.

"Uh-oh. We don't stand much of a chance in the row-boat," Jonas remarked to Eliza as she settled onto the seat, facing him. Sure enough, within sixty seconds of pulling away from shore, the other two teams had paddled so far ahead that there was no catching up to them. Jonas didn't just give up trying; he actually dragged his oars through the water.

"Why are you coming to a stop?" Eliza asked.

"Because I'd rather talk than race. It's more romantic."

"I agree." She nudged his knee with hers. "What would you like to talk about?"

"About how much I really and truly, genuinely love you," Jonas answered, grinning slyly.

"Neh." Eliza playfully shook her head. "I want to talk about how much *I* really and truly, genuinely love *you.*"

"Hmm." He scratched his jaw, pretending to think it over. "How about if we compromise and don't talk after all? Let's do this, instead."

Leaning forward, Jonas cupped Eliza's cheeks with both of his hands and pressed his lips to hers for a long, sweet kiss.

And then another. And another. And one more after that...

* * * * *

Dear Reader,

One of my favorite parts of writing Amish romance for Love Inspired™ is deciding which Bible verse to use for the epigraph. Sometimes I have a verse in mind as I'm writing the story. Other times, I'll do an online search of Scripture to expand my options. I'm always struck by how many verses seem to be the perfect fit. Literally words to live by. Choosing just one is rarely easy, but in this case, I knew even before I started the book which one I wanted to use (Colossians 3:13).

Researching and trying out Amish recipes is another part of writing these romance novels that I really enjoy. Blueberry buckle is one such recipe, and as I discovered, the cake's surface really does "buckle" under the weight of the berries and the crumbly topping. It's absolutely *appenditlich*!

Incidentally, one of my readers wrote to suggest I should include the recipes of Amish desserts I mention in my books on my website. I think that's a great idea, so please check there in the future if you're interested in baking a sweet Amish treat. Or else just stop by my site to drop me a line; I really do love hearing from you.

Blessings,
Carrie Lighte

Get 4 FREE REWARDS!

We'll send you 2 FREE Books plus 2 FREE Mystery Gifts.

FREE
Value Over
$20

Both the **Love Inspired®** and **Love Inspired®** Suspense series feature compelling novels filled with inspirational romance, faith, forgiveness, and hope.

YES! Please send me 2 FREE novels from the Love Inspired or Love Inspired Suspense series and my 2 FREE gifts (gifts are worth about $10 retail). After receiving them, if I don't wish to receive any more books, I can return the shipping statement marked "cancel." If I don't cancel, I will receive 6 brand-new Love Inspired Larger-Print books or Love Inspired Suspense Larger-Print books every month and be billed just $5.99 each in the U.S. or $6.24 each in Canada. That is a savings of at least 17% off the cover price. It's quite a bargain! Shipping and handling is just 50¢ per book in the U.S. and $1.25 per book in Canada.* I understand that accepting the 2 free books and gifts places me under no obligation to buy anything. I can always return a shipment and cancel at any time. The free books and gifts are mine to keep no matter what I decide.

Choose one: ☐ **Love Inspired**   ☐ **Love Inspired Suspense**
      Larger-Print   **Larger-Print**
      (122/322 IDN GNWC)   (107/307 IDN GNWN)

Name (please print)

Address   Apt. #

City   State/Province   Zip/Postal Code

Email: Please check this box ☐ if you would like to receive newsletters and promotional emails from Harlequin Enterprises ULC and its affiliates. You can unsubscribe anytime.

Mail to the **Harlequin Reader Service:**
IN U.S.A.: P.O. Box 1341, Buffalo, NY 14240-8531
IN CANADA: P.O. Box 603, Fort Erie, Ontario L2A 5X3

Want to try 2 free books from another series? Call 1-800-873-8635 or visit www.ReaderService.com.

*Terms and prices subject to change without notice. Prices do not include sales taxes, which will be charged (if applicable) based on your state or country of residence. Canadian residents will be charged applicable taxes. Offer not valid in Quebec. This offer is limited to one order per household. Books received may not be as shown. Not valid for current subscribers to the Love Inspired or Love Inspired Suspense series. All orders subject to approval. Credit or debit balances in a customer's account(s) may be offset by any other outstanding balance owed by or to the customer. Please allow 4 to 6 weeks for delivery. Offer available while quantities last.

LIRLIS22

LOVE INSPIRED

Stories to uplift and inspire

Fall in love with Love Inspired—
inspirational and uplifting stories of faith
and hope. Find strength and comfort in
the bonds of friendship and community.
Revel in the warmth of possibility and the
promise of new beginnings.

Sign up for the Love Inspired newsletter
at **LoveInspired.com** to be the first
to find out about upcoming titles,
special promotions and exclusive content.

CONNECT WITH US AT:

f Facebook.com/LoveInspiredBooks

🐦 Twitter.com/LoveInspiredBks

LISOCIAL2021